Reginald Spiffington

Mimsy Borogrove

Barking Mad

A Reginald Spiffington Mystery

Jamieson Ridenhour

To Holly —
Best wishes in Atlanta — 7/21/11

Smashing !!

[signature]

TYPECAST PUBLISHING

www.typecastpublishing.com

Please direct inquiries to:

Managing Editor
Typecast Publishing
7706 New LaGrange Road
Louisville, KY 40222

Library of Congress Control Number: 2011925308
ISBN: 978-0-9844961-2-9

Cover design by The Firecracker Press.
Illustrations by Ali LaRock.
Interior design by Kirkby Gann Tittle.

*For my mother, Brenda White, who introduced me to both
Agatha Christie and Lon Chaney, Jr.*

BARKING MAD

Chapter One

My story begins on a bright May morning. I say it was bright, and I have all assurances it was, though I myself only saw it filtered through the chocolate-colored drapes in my bedroom, where I was vainly trying to remain asleep. Bit of a blow-out the night before. Bit of a lie-in that morning was the logical next step, it seemed to me. Such dreamy plans were sadly not to be, however. I was not asleep, and it seemed increasingly likely I was not to have much of a lie-in.

I hear you even now asking, "Why?" Perhaps you are even so bold as to embellish your question into a rather ornate construction such as, "Why, oh why, Reginald, will the mysterious powers that govern this mad world not allow you such a bare necessity as a Friday morning lie-in?" And well you may ask. It seems monstrous that a hale and hearty young specimen such as myself should be required or expected to show his bleary-eyed face at the breakfast trough before eleven on a Friday. And yet, my friends and well-wishers. And yet.

The culprit, you'll soon discover (because I'm going to tell you) is that beastly instrument the telephone. You may argue the true culprit is the deucedly wicked person on the other end of the telephone who kept ringing my number that fateful May morning, three times before ten o'clock with no signs of taking a break for brunch, and you'd be right. But, having no foreknowledge of who the blighter was as I lay curled in a fetal position, pillows over my ears, I blamed the 'phone. Telephones have a dashedly evil jangle to them, like the infernal rattling of the Devil's key-ring, and at 9:45 in the a.m., well, I mean to say.

I could hear my man, Pelham, crossing the hall each time the devilish thing would go off, and then crossing back after telling the persistent little scamp I was still unavailable. It was only, as the poetically inclined might say, a matter of time before I would hear the soft-knuckled entreaty upon my chamber door. I steeled myself, as well as one can steel oneself in a silken night-shirt. The more I thought, and I use the term loosely when applying it to a Friday forenoon, the more I felt a surety as to the identity of the dastardly 'phone goblin. And that surety induced in the frame of Reginald Spiffington a chill as if gripped by the icy hand of what have you. The only chap of my acquaintance as unchari-tably bulldoggish about talking to someone when it becomes increasingly clear they are sleeping off a to-do is my aged and paternal grandfather, the not-so-Honorable Hammerthorpe Q. Spiffington the third.

An astute reader will have already surmised the character of my aged GF by simply dispatching the chore of getting through the man's name. Why anyone in this day and age would walk around weighted with that bundle of syllabic clap-trap I can-not imagine. And he will admit no nicknames—once in younger days I ventured to call him "Hammy" (as I was feeling rather chummy in that fleeting moment of insanity) and quickly found myself unable to sit down for nearly a fortnight. The other chaps in my year at Cambridge found no end of delight in this, but I took what could be called a dimmer view. At any rate, it seems to be the sole purpose of Hammy's life to torment me. This has often been through the withholding of funds (a tight hand at the purse strings is the old GF) or through the detailed and enraged recounting of any minor scrapes I may have gotten myself into over the weekend. As if I don't read the papers.

Lately, however, the not-so-Honorable has been taking a more focused tack, which is to say, the old what-do-you-call-him has decided that it's not enough for me to lead the sort of dissolute and dissipated life to which I've grown accustomed (and there I'm quoting the old dust bunny), and that I should perhaps (a word which has an altered definition when dropping from the mouth of the GF) think about settling down. All of which can be translated for those of us who speak and think in modern English to mean my oldest relative would like me to marry any one of a series of dry slices of toast which he feels compelled to parade in front of me like a cattle show. The latest one, Lady Mildred Spinoza, was supposed to have supped with me at Regentio's the night before, but did not. For that I can hardly blame the Lady Mildred; for all I know she made a valiant attempt to keep the date. I found it hard to see Regentio's from the armchair at my club where I happened to be at the appointed time. And before you point the self-righteous finger of whichever at me, I have to say, in my defense, that the woman keeps a toy poodle. Ah! You think differently now, I daresay.

Which is as much to say I expected a friendly ring from the old tree-root this morning to ask me what did I mean by and hadn't I ever thought of and what did I plan on and didn't I ever consider. And that is why I rolled disconsolately from my bed and embarked upon the Spiffington toilette well before my preferred time. Because I did, for the reasons I've rather laboriously mentioned, expect the soft-knuckled etc., etc.

And it came, patient reader, it came. No sooner had I laid aside the razor and knotted the ascot than I heard the unmistakable rap-tap-tap of Pelham at the boudoir door. I whipped open the aforementioned portal and held up a manicured hand.

"No need, Pelham, no need," I said with all the force of foreknowledge. "I know what you've come to tell me."

"Indeed, sir?" Pelham is not by nature a taciturn creature; he needs but little incentive to begin chattering away about all manner of things. But, befitting a first-rate gentleman's gentleman, he limits his syllables to the necessary in most instances. This is as it should be. For one thing, he is privy to a great deal of information that was properly kept in the auditory dark, if you see what I mean.

"Indeed, Pelham," I confirmed, "You've come to tell me that my grandfather, the not-so-Honorable Hammerthorpe Q.

Spiffington, has telephoned no less than three times this a.m., that he is of an irate disposition at present, and that he wants to know what the devil I mean by it all. No matter the effect this early-bird telephonic admonition will have on my health. I mean to say, if a man can't get the requisite seven hours, I don't know what all. I've a mind . . ."

"If I may, sir?"

"Oh, er, yes, Pelham?"

"I have indeed received three communications via the telephone this morning sir, but none of them originated from Judge Spiffington."

"Ah. I see. I shall then save my spleen, Pelham, rather than improperly vent it."

"Very good, sir."

"I'm sure the aged GF will give me ample cause at some time in the near future."

"There is certainly precedent to expect so, sir."

"Right ho. To breakfast then."

"Sir?"

"Yes, Pelham?"

"Would you like to know who did place three telephone calls to you this morning, sir?"

"Only if the news can be given to me over a rasher of bacon and two or three of your redoubtable eggs, Pelham."

"I feel I should first inform you, sir..."

"Tut, tut, my man. Starvation is at the very door. I feel weakened, Pelham, and nothing but the full English breaking of the fast will do it."

"As you wish , sir."

"And coffee would not be remiss, old boy."

"The brewing has already commenced, sir."

"Ah. You are a veritable jewel, Pelham."

"I have my moments, sir."

Thus it was that I was seated at the table in my little dining nook half an hour later, giving appreciative nose to the bacony wafts drifting from kitchenward, when I heard a ring at the bell. As Pelham was engaged, I went to the door myself. There I discovered Moony Huffsworthy, an old college chum whom I hadn't seen in a coon's age, assuming the coon is a beast with a life-span between two and four months, not counting a wave across the room at the Streatham's ball in March.

"Moony, old bean!" I expounded, thumping him on the back in a manly but affectionate manner, "What in the world brings you 'round these parts?"

Moony looked confused, but as that was a natural expression for him, I merely assumed the norm. "But," he said, removing his topcoat, "I thought you knew why I was coming."

"Don't be silly, old man. I'm not a mind reader. Come on in the dining room and talk to me over bacon. Pelham's just laying the final flourishes."

"But I 'phoned three times, Reggie. I had hoped you'd be ready to go."

"Go? Where are we going?" The food was waiting on the table, and Pelham had rather thoughtfully laid a place for Moony as well. I pulled a chair for the chum, napkined the neck and upper torso, and tucked in with a vigor that threatened my cuffs.

Moony seemed less interested in the plateful of heaven provided. He appeared, now that I got a good look at him between heaping forkfuls, downright gloomy. "I *had* hoped," said Moony, looking like his dog had been kidnapped, "you were going with me down to Father's place in the country for the weekend. I need help."

"Pelham!" I called between mouthfuls. "Pelham, might I have you for a moment?"

As is his wont when called, Pelham presented himself. "Yes, sir?"

"Pelham, my friend Moony tells me he telephoned three times this morning to invite me for a weekend in the country, and it seems he's expecting me to leave with him sort of nowish." I glanced at Moony for confirmation and was rewarded with a despondent nod. "Were you aware of this, Pelham?"

"I was aware of it, sir. It was I who took the calls."

"I see. And can you tell me, Pelham, why it is I am only now being informed of these communiqués? If, and I do mean if, 'communiqué' means what I think it does?"

Pelham paused for a moment and took in the scene. Moony

7

looked grief-stricken, and I was putting forth pretty heavily with the righteous indignation. "I do apologize, sir. I left the house soon after the third call to buy a newspaper and neglected to tell you about Mr. Huffsworthy's calls upon my return. It is an egregious error, and one which lay entirely at my own feet."

"I see, Pelham. Well, perhaps you will think twice about your duties before acting in so irresponsible a manner a second time. But because you've used a word like 'egregious' I think allowances can be made. That is all. Oh, and Pelham?" This last due to his turning to go.

"Yes, sir?"

"This is absurdly good coffee, Pelham. Another cup if you would."

"Very good, sir."

An astute reader may find fault with this brief interchange between employer and employee, but there you are. Can't let them run all over you, what?

My attention turned back to Moony, who looked even more despairing than before. "I say, Moony, what's with all this mucky long-facedness, eh? Can't be as bad as all that."

"Oh yes it can, Reggie. Without you there this weekend I don't know what I'll do. I'm at my wit's end."

Now, I love Moony as a brother. Best of the best, bosom what-do-you-call-it, all that. But it is the considered opinion of his nearest and dearest that reaching Moony's "wit's end" is at best a short walk and one in which you're unlikely to break a sweat. No disrespect intended. It's just that Moony Huffsworthy is readily upset and easily depressed, especially where there are members of the fairer sex involved. At this juncture in our *tête à tête* (if I might insert a bilingual colloquialism) I began to suspect the dainty and scented hand of one of the legions of pretty young things which Moony continually found himself drawn to. Not one to display a backbone of which he is not in possession, Archibald J. Huffsworthy (he also is weighted with syllables, you see, but is more accommodating in the nickname department) is lord and master of the unrequited romance. If there is a way in which Moony prefers to love, it is from afar. The last time he needed my "help," it was to ghost-write love sonnets to Esmeralda Watchcase, the daughter of one of my father's law colleagues. At the crucial moment, he collapsed under the weight of his own agitation and threw the sonnets in the Thames, completely oblivious to the nearly twenty-seven minutes of brow-beetling I had lavished upon them. Regarding the present circumstances, I suspected a woman was at the bottom of this well.

"Moony," I declaimed, "I suspect there is a woman at the bottom of this well."

Moony sighed. In fact, feel free to insert that sentence in front of anything Moony says in this story up until at least mid-way through chapter two. "Not just a woman, Reggie. *The* woman. I know I've been infatuated in the past . . ."

"You have," I agreed, which was on the order of agreeing that the Atlantic Ocean was damp or that Windsor Castle was roomy. "I seem to recall it."

". . . and I know that I may have even gone so far as to declare love in one or two cases."

"Well, old chap, four or five, perhaps, but we're all guilty at one time or another."

"No, Reggie, no more than two, honestly. Matilda Bakewater and Carissa Lipwell are the two tragic past loves of my life. And they pale in comparison to this."

"Okay, Moony old bean, whatever you say. My memories of Esmeralda Watchcase and Marisol O'Reilly the Irish soprano are more than likely skewed."

"I'd say so. Marisol O'Reilly indeed!"

"My mistake, Moony my lad, please forgive etc. etc. We won't even mention Martha Hathaway in the same breath as your current paramour."

"Ugh! Martha Hathaway? After the contemptible way she treated me at the Summer Concert at Albert Hall? Have you ever tried to extract a meerschaum from a sousaphone?"

"Not while under police detention, my good little Moony, as I seem to remember was the case in that particular instance. Unfortunate all around. But pray don't let me keep you from what you were saying. This new one true love of yours. . . ?"

Moony takes steering, but I've got the measure of the wheel.

"Oh, Reggie, she is a dream. She is a slight waif of a thing, but her eyes, Reggie! Her complexion! The nightingale trilling of her voice! She is an angel, Reggie, an absolute angel!"

I polished off my bacon and slid Moony's plate in front of the old knife and fork, preparatory to making a second run. Pelham's bacon and eggs are just the thing, really. "And what, pray tell, is the name of this seraphic creature alighted from the celestial firmament? If indeed 'firmament' is the word I want?"

"Her name," crooned Moony, doing his best impression of a rapturous choir, "is Arabella Biscuit."

Good as the eggs and b were, I still felt it appropriate to choke. "Arabella Biscuit? The daughter of Sir Lionel Biscuit, bart.?"

"That's the one," said Moony, and the light had positively gone out of his eyes. He looked as dejectedly what-do-you-mean-to-say as any fellow I've had the misfortune to know. "It's the father that's the problem."

Long story short, then. Sir Lionel Biscuit, bart., is one of the nastiest pieces of unshaped clay I've ever been unfortunate enough to hear of. My aged GF has talked of him many times. A brutish bulldog of a man, with a mustache like the handlebars of a motorbike and a head like a live mortar round. Effusively bad-tempered and prone to senseless violence against those in the vicinity, this waste of oxygen had one great weakness—he adored his daughter Arabella. As far as protective fathers go, Sir Lionel had a monopoly to the extent it violated American anti-trust laws. I mean to say. I had heard stories of Sir Lionel losing what for lack of a more apt term I'll call his "cool" over a duke's son paying compliments to Arabella. I can only imagine how he'd react to love-making from one as unaccomplished and awkward as Moony Huffsworthy.

No one was more acutely, even painfully, aware of this fact than Moony himself. His father had invited the Biscuits to Huffsworthy Hall for the weekend, a turn of events one would be tempted to say was both fortuitous and hopeful, but Moony failed to feel up to it. There were other guests coming in, drawn by the comforts of the Hall and no doubt by the culinary expertise of the Huffsworthy chef, Dobbins. Moony felt if I were also in attendance, then perhaps I might help him press his suit?

My first inclination was to let my bosom pal know in no uncertain language that if I played Cyrano de Bergerac to his whats-his-name many more times I might actually begin growing my nose out. Upon reflection, however, I looked more kindly on the proposition. In point of fact, I adored Dobbins' cooking to the point of idolatry, and there was always a fair spot of hunting or tennis to be had at Huffsworthy Hall, a grand old home with much to recommend it in the comforts department. And, to be completely honest, it seemed more than likely my grandfather would eventually pick up the 'phone to remonstrate, because the man simply lives to remonstrate, and what a treat to have an elsewhere to which I might abscond.

Thus did I find myself saying, "Of course, Moony, old boy. Nothing I wouldn't do. No reason to thank me, think nothing of it, always willing to sacrifice for a friend. Why don't you head on down, and as soon as Pelham can throw some things of mine in the car, we'll be on our way. See you there late this afternoon?"

Moony was absurdly grateful, which seemed earned, and in two shakes I had let Pelham know of our new weekend plans and had gone upstairs to change into my travelling togs. Pelham had packed the standard suits and accoutrement, and had gone to pull the car around. I was stuffing my shaving kit with the shaving caboodle when he returned.

"Ah, Pelham. The car is, I take it, ready?"

"Yes, sir. Only one thing awaits your attending before we disembark."

"And what would that be, Pelham?"

"The telephone, sir. It was ringing as I came in from the street. It's your grandfather."

"Does he sound in a remonstrating mood?"

"He did apply several adjectives to your name which are not commonly deployed when one is feeling satisfied with the subject to which they are applied, sir."

"I see. Could you nip down and let him know I've been killed in a knife fight?"

"Yes, sir."

No reason to spoil the start of a lovely weekend. I mean to say.

Chapter Two

Huffsworthy Hall is one of those places tourists would happily pay too much to walk through, and touch the tapestries even though there are explicit signs posted asking them not to. Except that Lord Huffsworthy, owner in residence and father to our boy Moony, would never allow common tourists to tramp around the place. A great spacious palace, Huffsworthy Hall also sported a large park and grounds that let onto a sizable piece of woodland suitable for hunting. Tennis and croquet could be had on the grounds themselves, an extensive library was available indoors, and as I've said the food was five-star cuisine of a kind unrivalled in the country. Apologies if I sound like an ad pamphlet; Huffsworthy Hall makes me wax poetic to the point that I could be interred in Madame Tussaud's. I simply love the place.

It is therefore somewhat unfortunate that Lord Huffsworthy does not, by any stretching of the accepted definition of the word, love me. There are even times when he might be said to have evidenced an avowed dislike of me, though I've personally never given him cause. I mean, things break all the time, and I can't be expected to know whose niece is whose. I wouldn't say Lord Huffsworthy is a troll on the order of my grandfather, but he's certainly training for the pros, if you see what I mean.

Still, in a paradise such as Huffsworthy Hall there are ample opportunities for avoiding the old persimmon except at meal times, and it is then that Dobbins' delectable performances overshadow any little irritations such as curse-laden aspersions or subpoenas. So it was with decidedly high spirits that I set off from my Regent's Park digs soon after lunch on Friday morning, Pelham at the wheel of the roadster, and my hair not actually streaming in the breeze but thinking about it mightily. The sky was a crisp blue and the few clouds were minding their own business and not gumming up the works for those of us who like our weather on the dry side of damp. All in all, I'd describe my mood and manner as effervescent and jovial, and with an elbow on the window ledge and a cigarette twixt the lips I felt as good as dash it.

I was just telling Pelham I had planned a spot of hunting in the evening, as the moon would be nearly full and there must be some sort of bird or other to be shot. And then, in a maddeningly quick blink of an eye—I mean an eye that was rapidly blinking, as if incommoded by a lash—we were swerving to avoid a bloody great horse. We had come around a bend to find the thing standing stock still in the middle of the roadway, and before you could say, "Egad, a large horse is in the roadway!" we had come to ground in what for lack of a better epithet I'll call a ditch.

It's no great surprise this particular horse was disinclined to move, for seated on its back was a man whose bulk was scarcely less than that of the beast who bore his burden. I mean to say this chap was strapping; everything about him was positively bulging. I felt some trepidation about the seams of his jacket as he swung himself off the huge steed, which still had not moved, and approached us. Pelham and I had by this point extricated ourselves from the stranded roadster and were surveying the situation. I was miffed, I'll admit, but at least the walking bit of masonry had the decency to come over to apologize. I looked up at his blonde edifice and held out my hand.

"I say. Bit of a shock, what? Never fear, however. Due to the swift and certain steerage of my man Pelham here, we are none the worse for wear."

"What the devil are you playing at," came the inexplicable reply, "nearly running down my horse and me?" As I looked more clearly at our new acquaintance, I could see he was breathing heavily, not apparently as a result of exertion (he had after all merely been sitting on an unmoving horse) but from strong emotion. What's more, I took his bark-like speech to mean this emotion was directed largely at Pelham and me. I am of an equable and uncontentious nature in general, especially when the other party is of a size nearly twice my own and ostensibly built of granite, but I am not one to politely take being looked at askance. My own emotions were rather hotter than usual. My dander, I must disclose, was up.

"Look here, my good man," I said, meeting his gaze as well as I could from my lower vantage point, "what about that horse?" The interrogative stumped him. "Whazzat?" he asked. Clearly an intellect, but onward we go. "What about my horse?"

"Well, it seems a public road such as this may not be the prime venue for a stationary nag like that one. I have been nearly killed, and my car is trapped in this ditch. It's a dashed rum thing, and I hold you accountable!"

"Nag?" he repeated dangerously, seizing on the least important portion of my speech as I saw it. "My Abercrombie a nag?"

"Well, it's hardly a sprightly animal, is it? I mean to say, we all but flung a roadster at the poor thing's head and it still stands there as if it's been fly-papered."

Perhaps you'll think I was being unfair, but the beast in question remained like a horse-shaped log with neither a twitch or whinny. It was a big Shire horse with long hair over its hooves; perhaps that made it wary to move for fear of treading on its own foot-locks. At all events, I may have misstepped by insulting the poor brute, because the other poor brute, *vis-a-vis* the mountainous cretin in front of me, seemed to take it amiss. He swelled noticeably, and his face darkened from red to a plum color that looked distinctly unhealthy—for me, I should say. Without a word he turned and strode back to his horse.

"I say, Pelham?"

"Yes, sir?" Pelham had been engaged in attempted rescue of the roadster, which was unwilling to reverse itself from where it lay ensconced, one might almost say happily, in the ditch.

"I fear, Pelham, that we are about to be horse-whipped." This was not hyperbole. Our equestrian ogre had retrieved an actual horse-whip and was making his way back across the roadway with it.

"It appears so, sir."

"Have you any suggestions, Pelham? I do not hesitate to declare myself at a loss."

"Yes, sir. You will note that the road loops here around the field which is bordered by this ditch."

"I had noticed that Pelham, albeit in a rather peripheral way. You know, I'm not sure a geography lesson is quite the thing I was going for."

"Get into the car sir."

"Oh. Right ho." And into the car we got. Mr. Horsey had reached us by that point, but seemed reluctant to horse-whip us while we were in the car. I say "seemed," but he himself confirmed this theory by bluntly saying, "Oi. Get out of that bloody car, you two!"

Pelham, instead of complying with this crudely phrased request, put the car in gear and pressed the throttle. Off we shot across the field, spraying plants which in the absence of true knowledge I'll call wheat, though barley is a good guess as well, in all directions. By the time we had neatly run through the other side of the field and back onto the road, which did indeed loop around in a most helpful manner, our horse-whipping nemesis had sprinted (if such can be credited in a man the size of the Queen Mary) back to the steed and remounted. The Clydesdale then moved for the first time—he bolted forward through the field behind us at an angle, galloping like anything, and came out, because in a wheat field bloody great horses are apparently swifter on the ground than roadsters, ahead of us. The blighter was "heading us off at the pass" as they say in American cowboy pictures.

I said something apropos here, such as, "Yikes!" or, "Egad!" And though I don't want you thinking ill of Pelham's driving abilities, I am forced by narrative responsibilities to report that for the second time in ten minutes, Pelham swerved the car. He swerved like his life depended on it. Good job, too. The car did not veer ditchward on this second swerving excursion, but made a neat semi-circle around the advancing centaur and continued along the highway. This rather nifty move spooked the poor beast, and looking backwards over my shoulder I was greeted by the gratifying sight of Mr. Horsewhip being thrown from his perch and landing in what I hope was a patch of brambles.

"Quite an adventure, eh, Pelham?" I could see my man had what nearly amounted to a slight smile on his face.

"Yes, sir. I trust our stay at Huffsworthy Hall will be less eventful."

"I trust it will, Pelham. Still, makes the blood run quick, what?"

"Yes, sir. Most invigorating."

We arrived at the hall at about four-thirty in the afternoon, none the worse for our brief flirtation with the rogue cavalryman. Pelham took the car around to the garage whilst I wandered up the steps and into the front hall, where I was greeted by Bugsby, the Huffsworthy butler, who took my things and reminded me of my usual room. I thanked him and inquired after young Moony. Hearing he was in the library, I sauntered across the marbled foyer, if I may be so French, and made my entrance through the oaken portals of that book-lined cavern.

Moony was not alone, and I immediately felt my already high hopes for the weekend soar into the low-lying clouds. I knew there would be other guests, but I had never dreamed that my luck would turn out so, well, lucky. For who should I find in the library, holding court to young Moony Huffsworthy on the merits of detective fiction, but celebrated lady crime novelist Mimsy Borogove? She looked as she always did, gauzily clad in a diaphanous gown, her coppery tresses pulled back from her noble forehead and flashing green eyes. I had not seen Mimsy in several months, but had spent a fair amount of time gazing at the photo of her on the dust jacket of her latest novel, *Murder in the Soup*.

"Mimsy," I said, "what an unexpected thingy! I'm simply delighted. You know, I adored *Murder in the Soup*! Had me guessing right until the end. I had my money on the cream of celery; imagine my shock to discover it was the tomato!"

"Reggie, darling!" She always called me darling. She took my hands and made kissy movements near my cheeks. "How lovely! But surely my little plaything didn't really fool you? There were so many clues, darling. I felt that one embarrassingly obvious, but the publishers *will* have a manuscript every eight months."

"Wasn't obvious to me. Should have been, I guess. It is always tomato soup, isn't it? Tomato soup is so dreadfully eternal. I'm simply mad about your books. Are you working on anything new?"

Mimsy lit a cigarette in a long tortoiseshell holder. "Oh always, darling, always. The new one is half finished. It's called *Murder by Bratwurst*, possibly my finest whodunit yet. I'm working this weekend, actually, between whatever frivolity Moony can conjure up for us. Or, now that you're here, darling, whatever else *we* can come up with."

This is exactly the sort of thing that happens at Huffsworthy Hall, and exactly the reason I'm always keen to visit in spite of Lord Huffsworthy's marked and irrational dislike of me. I had been infatuated with Mimsy Borogove for a good eight months—simply ages!—and here she was discussing an assignation. Or perhaps she was suggesting tennis. But, by jingo, I was up for either. I could feel my face smiling for all it was worth.

Then I looked at Moony, whose own face had dropped so low it endangered the shine of the oaken floorboards. I felt a twinge, my good readers, a decided twinge. It was no doubt bad form to be shamelessly flirting with Mimsy Borogove when Moony's own love life hung so delicately in the balance. And since it looked unlikely I could ditch Moony without a fair amount difficulty, I suggested we meet again at the dinner table. Mimsy went up to her room to do some writing—she was planning to finish her novel by the end of the month and didn't want to waste a second, sweet little worker bee that she was—and I asked Moony if any of the other guests had arrived. He told me Arabella and her father were in the drawing room having pre-dinner drinks and talking with Reynaldo MacGregor, Scottish-Italian tenor with the National Opera and frequent Huffsworthy visitant.

"Well then, lead on MacDuff!" said I, dusting off the Shakespeare in my ebullience, "Let's get a gander at this dream girl of yours. I might as well get on the job, so to speak."

I followed Moony into the drawing room, a silken affair whose decoration had been overseen by Moony's mother soon before she passed away, possibly in response to the effect of the wallpaper against the sofas. Oscar Wilde's last words were supposedly "Either the wallpaper goes or I do," and perhaps Lady Huffsworthy surveyed her unfortunate slapdashery in the Hall's drawing room and chose the latter course. It's just as well the rest of the house and grounds were so utterly smashing, because the drawing room was a sign of the decline of the empire as far as I could tell.

Seated on one of the god-awful sofas was the present object of Moony's affection. I had seen Arabella Biscuit once before, but hadn't been particularly interested at the time. Circs being what they were I now assessed the young lady with the goggles of attention, as you might put it. She was pretty in a vacant sort of way, with colorless hair and watery blue eyes. She looked, to be perfectly frank, like an overcooked noodle. "Isn't she like nothing else on this earth?" breathed Moony in my ear. I love Moony like a close relative, as I've said, but on the comparatively brief list of chaps I want breathing in my ear, he gets nary a mention. Not a tick.

Arabella was sitting, as I believe I have said, on a hideous sham of a settee, listening to her father expound to Reynaldo MacGregor on the proper approach to the American stock market. Sir Lionel Biscuit, bart., was an overstuffed armchair of a man who smoked immoderately large cigars composed of some magical stuff that simultaneously boasted enormous about-to-fall columns of ash while at the same time never growing any shorter. The contrast of his ruddy skin with the blinding white of his mustachios (I wondered if he bleached them) reminded one of nothing so much as drawings of the Walrus from Mr. Carroll's *Alice* books. He spoke loudly and with confidence, and he looked as if he smelled of anchovies.

Reynaldo MacGregor, tenor with the National Opera, needs no description, and indeed has none.

Everyone looked up as we entered: Arabella demurely, Sir Lionel aggressively, and Signor MacGregor nondescriptly. I was heartened by Arabella's demurring, which seemed inspired by at least a glimmer of the reciprocal toward my old school chum, but this apparent sign of fortune was mitigated by the way in which Sir Lionel glowered. At a glance I knew I had my work cut out for me, if I may venture a sartorial metaphor at such a juncture.

Advancing with my winningest smile (three-quarter teeth, dimples engaged but not fully flexed, eyes merrily a-sparkle) I said, "Ah, right ho! Sir Lionel Biscuit, I believe? Reginald Spiffington at your service." Initial success as the baronet took my proffered hand of brotherly what-have-you. "I believe you know my grandfather, Hammerthorpe Q. Spiffington, the High Court judge?"

"Ah, yes," Sir Lionel said, fishily wafting at me and puffing on the magic ash-candle between his teeth, "crafty old fox, your grandfather. I knew him in the war. Can't say as I have any use for the man. He was a rat in '17, and I'll warrant he's a rat now."

Nothing worse than having the truth about your relatives spoken in public. Even given the man's repulsive façade, I was taken aback by his audacity. It was a good job that I caught sight of Moony, cringing in the corner between the French windows and the armoire, or else I would have defended the Spiffington honor with all the vim and vigor of a freshly sharpened tongue. I chose instead to bite the barbed missile, and continued beaming at the odious little man. "Yes, well, he speaks as highly of you. Lovely to see you here, so good of Lord Huffsworthy to have you. And this must be your radiant daughter Arabella, of whom I've heard raptures from Moon—from Mr. Huffsworthy." Here I gallantly took the Noodle's hand and pressed the lips. The young ingénue blushed, calling to mind a sunburned albino.

"Humpf," grunted Sir Lionel. He actually did—he said, "Humpf." "I can't imagine that young milksop could know enough about my Arabella to give you anything like accurate information. What are you doing over there, anyway?" This to Moony, who had sort of wedged himself partially behind the armoire in the extremity of his terror. "Come out from behind that armoire, you great booby! What a bloody child!" Sir Lionel's voice, it should be here noted, rather suggested a foghorn placed within three to seven feet of the head. It actually tightened the knot of my ascot when he spoke.

With Arabella Biscuit watching expectantly, Moony attempted

to disengage himself from the position into which he had squidged, but for a moment it appeared the worst had happened and he was well and truly stuck. His face turned colors and he strained with what must be assumed to be all or most of his might, and yet there he stayed. I moved to help him, but just as I completed my purposeful stride he popped from the corner—literally, audibly popped—like a champagne cork at an election night concession party. The force thus generated, whether centrifugal, kinetic, eccentric, or detective I have not the wherewithal to name, propelled the unfortunate blighter halfway across the room where he tripped on a paisley ottoman before collapsing at full-length upon the Persian rug. At once he rolled sort of diagonally forward, leapt to his feet and, with a timorous and despairing glance over the shoulder at Arabella, bolted from the room.

In the absence of Moony's triathlon to capture the interest, all three of the room's other occupants then turned their eyes to me, as if expecting me to do cartwheels while whistling "I'm Just Wild About Harry." I chose to disappoint.

"Well," I said in voice which held not a trace of the chalant, "it was certainly lovely to meet you all. I must go and change for dinner. I trust we shall continue this delightful little cohort over the Huffsworthy board this evening." And I left the room, still unsure of the definition of "cohort." Work, as I say, cut out for me.

Pelham had laid out my dinner clothes by the time I got to my room, and I mulled the problem of Moony and Arabella as I pulled on the soup and fish.

"Pelham," I said, "I am mulling the problem of Moony and Arabella."

"Indeed, sir?" said Pelham, brushing down my jacket. "And have you sighted any conclusions?"

"I have not."

"I see, sir. What are the major obstacles?"

"The major obstacle is Sir Lionel Biscuit, bart.," I said, straightening my tie.

"He objects to Mr. Huffsworthy as a suitor?"

"He objects to Moony on general grounds as person who exists in the world."

"I see."

"I'm not sure how to proceed at this juncture, Pelham. But I do see the need to separate Arabella from her father. She didn't seem averse to the old boy, if I could get the two of them alone somewhere."

"Perhaps you should invite Sir Lionel play tennis tomorrow."

I looked with wonder on the man. "Do you think it's that easy? Can someone the size and shape of Sir Lionel Biscuit actually play a game of tennis without damage to self and court?"

"He is certainly rotund, sir. But by all accounts he is also competitive. His butler suggested to me earlier this evening that Sir Lionel fancies himself athletic."

"His butler?"

"Yes, sir. A Mr. Smythe. He has been in Sir Lionel's employ for many years, and informs me the baronet becomes more adamant of his physical prowess on the court and field even as he grows less able to commit athletics."

"Crumbs, Pelham! Crikey and begod! You are invaluable. This tennis scheme of yours will work like anything. And, I'll be able to easily win a game of tennis in front of Mimsy Borogove! Look frightfully manly of me, what?"

"It is, if I may say so sir, positive on all sides of the equation."

"Thank you, Pelham. You have once again proven your worth in spades!"

I arrived in the dining room spot on seven, and found myself neither the first nor the last guest to do so. Arabella and her father were there, but Mimsy was not. Moony was at the table, torn between gazing somewhat dreamily at Arabella Biscuit and flinching violently whenever Sir Lionel lifted a cup or shifted his arm.

"Hi ho!" I burbled.

"Hullo, Reggie," said Moony, and Arabella smiled weakly at me.

Sir Lionel barked, "Oh, it's only you. I thought perhaps it was Fitchly."

I seated myself. "It is only I," I admitted. "Who, pray, is Fitchly?"

"Friend of mine. Coming down for the weekend as well.

Jolly good man, very close with my Arabella. Name of Fitchly Skorjenhensen."

"Of Scandinavian descent, is Mr. Skorjenhensen?"

"Swedish extraction, I believe, though he's as English as you or me. Nothing funny or foreign about him. A good man."

Pelham will maintain there is no such thing as coincidence, but then something like this happens to put a run in those trousers. At that moment, a strange man entered the dining room, and Sir Lionel stood and said, "Ah, Fitchly. Just talking about you. Come in, come in."

When I used the word "strange" in that last sentence, it was unfortunately in the sense of "odd" or "bizarrely large," not in the expected sense of "unfamiliar." For this Fitchly Skorjenhensen revealed himself to be none other than the hulking horseman who attempted bodily injury to Pelham and me on the highway three hours previous. Had you a sufficiently large feather, you could have tried to knock me down with it. I would have promptly taken it from you and hidden myself behind it.

Fitchly Skorjenhensen muscled through the doorway, nodding at Sir Lionel and then smiling in a much-too-friendly way at Arabella (who received it not quite in the manner in which it was extended, I'm happy to say). He had not yet seen me. I eyed the doors, but was prevented from executing my plan (which had been to run very fast out the French doors and into the woods where I would hide until dark) by the arrival of Signor MacGregor and Mimsy Borogove, who arrived separately, one at each door. My discovery was delayed while Sir Lionel introduced both of the newcomers to Fitchly Skorjenhensen, and then, as the table simply groaned under the weight of laden platters and tureens, all parties sat down to tuck in.

"Shall we not," said Mimsy, who even in the presence of the mountainous Swede looked radiant and clever, "wait on Lord Huffsworthy?" The question served to momentarily break Moony's gaze away from the Noodle.

"Oh, daddy's not here," said Moony. "He should be back tomorrow mid-morning, but sent his regrets for this evening. Business up in London."

"Oh, that's too bad," returned Mimsy. "Well, at least we can be thankful for having Mr. Spiffington here to entertain us." And here she turned the full light of her insinuation into my face. I would have felt it as the sunlight after rain to be so honored, were it not that Mimsy's flirtatious overtures drew the attention of the entire table to me, and that Fitchly Skorjenhensen was at that table. He saw me fully for the first time. There was a brief moment where it looked possible he had not recognized me, so well-turned out was I.

Alas, such are the stuff of dreams. A thin filament began to glow in the low wattage of Fitchly Skorjenhensen's skull, and within a scant fifteen seconds he knew exactly who I was. Being that we were no longer in the wilds of a field bordered roadway, it is to be expected that his reaction was subdued. Expectations are fickle things, really.

"What in the bloody hell is *he* doing here?" he roared, leaping to his full and considerable height and pulling the tablecloth with him, as he had clutched it in an effort to crush something immediately upon registering my identity. "What the *bloody* blazes is that cove doing *here*?" Not quite fair asking again, not having given anyone a chance to answer the first time.

"He is a guest here," Mimsy said, bless her sparkling heart. "What the devil are you so upset about? Please let go of the tablecloth!"

"He's a madman," shouted Skorjenhensen. "He tried to run me down as I rode over here this afternoon. Look at the cuts! Look at the bruises!" Indeed, the huge man's visage was a network of fresh scars, rendering his face even more like that of a Neanderthal than even Mother Nature had granted. Score a point for the bramble bush.

"Now just a moment," I interjected at this point. I felt fairly safe with Mimsy's support. And I had the table between me and my accuser. "I did nothing of the sort. If people are going to plant horses in the middle of roads, then it is to be expected there's a certain risk incurred. And then you tried to horse-whip my man and me. If anyone has a complaint it should be—"

"My horse Abercrombie will never get over it! He's all a-tremble now in the stables! You're a madman!" And with this he started to come around the table at me.

I grabbed a candle-stick and prepared to defend myself. "Have at you, you cretin!" I said. I'm not sure from what adventure story I appropriated the phrase, but circumstances seemed to warrant it, and I must admit it delivered a certain amount of satisfaction.

Luckily for me, because no matter how well-spoken I was surely the small dog in a bullfight, Sir Lionel intervened by putting a hand on the brute's arm. "Now, now, Fitchly. Let's be civil about this. Have a seat. I'm sure that whatever happened between you and Mr. Spiffington was a misunderstanding." He eyed me shrewdly as he said this, and I felt it clearly that Sir Lionel was not preventing fisticuffs due to any concern for my welfare.

Fitchly Skorjenhensen reluctantly sat down again. "Misunderstanding, my eye," he said. "Bloke drove his car right at me, and then drove off through a field! Had his manservant at the wheel. Madmen, both of them!"

"Well, that seems like strange behavior. Through a field you say?" Sir Lionel eyed me again as he lifted his soup spoon.

Moony slowly recovered from the threat of violence and turned to me. "But did you really, Reggie old boy? Drove off through a field?"

"The field was the most expeditious way of escaping," I said. "The man was trying to horse-whip us!"

"He tried to run me down, and he insulted my horse!" Skorjenhensen rose again, but was once again restrained by Sir Lionel.

"Now, now. Eat your soup. Everything seems calm now. I'm sure Mr. Spiffington has an explanation for trying to run you down."

"Of course he does," said Mimsy. "Tell them, Reggie."

"I didn't try to run him down! He was right in the middle of the road! Look, I wasn't even driving . . . !"

Sir Lionel winked at Arabella. "Drinks a bit, I shouldn't wonder," he said. Arabella looked at me wide-eyed, never having seen a real live lush, I suppose. "Makes you wonder about the sort of people who would consort with drunkards," her father continued, looking meaningfully at Moony. Arabella turned her watery blues on him as well.

"Oh, Daddy," she said in an undertone, "you don't think—"

"I do indeed, my sugarplum. I do indeed. Aren't you fortunate that Fitchly has turned up to protect you?"

Moony dropped his spoon, stood up, and said, "Reggie, might I have a word with you?" He left the room.

"Ah. I'll be back in a jiff," I said to Mimsy, who winked at me.

Moony was in the hallway, pacing back and forth in an agitated manner. "Reggie! You are supposed to be helping me!"

"I aim to help you, Moony old boy."

"Well, you've been here less than three hours and you've already gotten me further away from Arabella than I was before. And that wasn't very close!"

"Well, surely I can't help her father being an ass! And who is that pugilistic horse-lover? Why would your father let someone like that into Huffsworthy Hall? The man talks like a music hall barker! Manners of a rabid mastiff."

"He's Sir Lionel's right-hand man, so to speak. They are everywhere together. And he's got designs on my Arabella." He looked close to tears. Again.

"The man is a brute. But look, don't you think we should be at the table? Surely we've reached the credit limit on odd for the day. Let's do go back in. I haven't even tried Dobbins' soup!"

"What, exactly, is your plan?" Moony had stopped and now looked challengingly at me. Or near to, anyway. Moony has had little practice in challenging.

"My plan had been to play a game of tennis with Sir Lionel."

"What? That's absurd. How will that help me?"

"The idea, and it was Pelham's idea, not mine, was to occupy the father for forty-five minutes or so to give you time alone with Arabella. Sir Lionel's competitive streak would guarantee his attention."

"Oh. That's brilliant!"

"Yes. Too bad we'll have to come up with something else."

"Why?"

"Well, I can hardly play tennis with the man now. He called me a drunkard in front of the whole table. Principles, all that."

"Reggie, you must! I must have time with Arabella. I must confess my love!"

26

"Moony, old bean, I really don't see—"

"Reggie! How much do you enjoy coming here and eating Dobbins' food?"

"It's among the most rarefied pleasures I am privy to, Moony, but—"

"And if I pine away and die, how often do you think my father will invite you?"

"If you what?"

"I shall pine, Reggie. I daresay it's upon me even now."

"Oh good lord. You are a unique animal, Moony. All right then."

"All right then, what?"

"All right then I'll play a ruddy game of ruddy tennis with Sir ruddy Lionel. Now, please, my soup will be positively icy."

We returned to the table. Possibly my soup was icy, possibly it was not. As it had been removed to make room for the next course I was hardly in a position to judge. I shot a glance at Moony, and then smiled at Mimsy, who looked at me enquiringly. Arabella looked at Moony, and then blinked nervously at Fitchly Skorjenhensen. Sir Lionel squinted at me and Moony, and Skorjenhensen looked at Arabella. Signor MacGregor looked at his plate, a wine glass neatly balanced between thumb and pointer.

We were happily interrupted in our little peering party by the arrival of the entrée, a braised lamb with mint and new potatoes. The smell of the thing made my heart flutter, and I thanked the gilded what-have-you that I could be near the place Dobbins cooked. I realized any sacrifice was worth this. So I bit the proverbial bullet.

"Would you like to play tennis tomorrow morning, Sir Lionel?"

The man looked as if I'd asked him to shave a fish. "Eh? What the devil did you say?"

"I asked if you'd like to play tennis tomorrow, say mid-morning? The weather looks as if it will hold, and the courts here are among the best I've had the pleasure of." A pause while Sir Lionel sized me up and wondered what I was playing at. "Unless, " I continued, "you don't feel up to it? I know I'm much younger, but I'm sure to be a little rusty." In for a penny, as they say.

The baronet made a sound like an emphysmatic shih tzu, which I believe should technically be called a laugh. "Oh, that's very amusing. I'd be delighted to meet you on the court in the morning. Let's say ten o'clock? That should be early enough for everyone to still be sober. And if I might suggest an enlargement of the party?"

"I beg your pardon?"

"I know Fitchly here likes a good game of tennis." At this Fitchly Skorjenhensen looked up, confused, with a string of lamb hanging from one ponderous canine. "And I imagine growing up at Huffsworthy Hall must have put young Archibald near the court once or twice." Moony looked away from Arabella, alarmed. "I propose," said Sir Lionel, "a doubles match amongst the four of us. You and Mr. Huffsworthy on one side of the net and Mr. Skorjenhensen and I on the other."

I was trapped. Couldn't think of a way out of it. Looked in vain for Pelham, who was not to be glimpsed. Moony's eyes bulged like Fitchly's upper arms. "Right ho," I said. "Smashing!"

"Does that sound agreeable to you, Mr. Huffsworthy?" asked the baronet.

"Quite!" squeaked Moony. He looked like he might faint.

Dinner was exquisite. I found the ability to appreciate the delicate nuance of flavor that Dobbins brings to every joyful nibblet, despite Moony continually giving me meaningful glances and Sir Lionel elbowing Fitchly and nodding in my direction every time I refilled my wine glass. What are such concerns when lost in the epicurean splendor of a truly gifted chef? My unwarranted high spirits were further hoisted by the undeniable attention of Mimsy Borogove, who was giving me, if I may put it so crudely, the eye.

Moony and I chose not to linger with cigars at table, and left the room soon after the ladies. Reynaldo MacGregor was telling a story about his Italian aunt back home in Aberdeen when we beat our retreat. Moony followed me into the library and closed the oaken portal.

"What do you mean by it, Reggie? I mean to say!"

"Hold the proverbial horses, Moony old chum. I had nothing to do with it. You heard the old toad propose a doubles match. What should I have said?"

"That I had a war injury! That my foot was broken! That I have a deep-seated phobia of tennis stemming from when I was but a child and my father berated me for losing a singles match to Freddie Highwater!"

"That last one was rather specific."

"Yes, well."

"Look, Moony. You want me to make you look palatable in front of Arabella Biscuit, correct?"

"Yes, of course. But—"

"But me no buts. How would it have looked if you had scampered away from an athletic challenge from her father and the man who her father clearly has picked out as the one for her? Not so manly, eh?"

"I suppose not."

"There you have it. Tomorrow, we shall either put it to the beastly pair, thus demonstrating your great worth and prowess to Arabella, or else we shall be used as mops to clean the court, in which case Arabella will feel sympathetic tenderness towards you for being bullied by a great ox like Fitchly Skorjenhensen. Either way, you gain points with the girl of your dreams!"

"Well, when you put it like that." He brightened considerably. "You really think it will turn out like that?"

"Of course I do. I have immense experience in the ways and wiles of women, Moony."

"And you didn't make that up just now to cover a blunder?"

"Moony, we know not when the muse of truth comes upon us. Ours is but to something something and woo the maiden fair."

At that moment the door opened and Arabella came in. She went directly to Moony and took his hand. Her watery blue eyes stared up into his and she said, rather breathlessly, "I think you're so brave!" Then she blushed furiously and fled the room.

Moony stood like a man in a trance for twenty-five seconds. Then he grabbed my hand and shook it as if he wanted to take it home with him. "Reggie, you're a wonder!" he said, and then he left as well.

I was feeling rather good about myself. I wandered back towards the dining room to see if there happened to be any wine left in the carafe, and on the way encountered Mimsy Borogove coming out of the drawing room. She pulled me conspiratorially aside and whispered in my ear.

"Reggie, darling—I've got a picnic basket set aside in the front hall."

I was happy to be alone with her at last, but couldn't quite follow the gist. "Oh," I said. "Good for you!"

"No, silly person," she giggled. "I have a picnic basket set aside with food and wine for *two*. Do you understand me now?"

A light dawned in my brain and elsewhere. "Oh! When and where?"

"There's a clearing in the woods south of the fountain on the lawn. You can't miss it, as they say. If you bring a blanket there at, say, nine o'clock, I'll bring the basket."

"Shall I know you in the dark, my dear?" I can be so suave when pressed.

"There's a full moon tonight, darling. We'll have all the light we need." And she disappeared into the drawing room.

It was going to be a very interesting night indeed.

Chapter Three

I'll admit to whistling a jaunty tune as I made my way into the smoking room. I was unconcerned that I would most probably be sharing the place with Sir Lionel and his Frankenstein's monster of a sidekick. Reginald Spiffington was a master of the world around him, particularly in the arena of romance. An assignation with a prominent female novelist, and matchmaker to Moony and the Noodle. Not bad for a brisk three hours work. I was feeling pretty good about old Reggie as I entered the smoking room.

All the men were there. Moony was sitting in an armchair between Signor MacGregor and a stuffed badger. Sir Lionel Biscuit, bart., and Fitchly Skorjenhensen were playing billiards at the far end of the room. The clack of balls made a companionable what-do-you-call-it as I filled a tumbler with scotch and splashed a dab of soda.

"Drinking again, Spiffington?" said Sir Lionel from beneath the head of a wart hog across the billiard table.

"Right-o, Sir Lionel! Something about you just inspires me," I said. I daresay I said it saucily, so filled was my head with images of Mimsy Borogove's coppery locks and emerald eyes. "Looking at the two of you there, what can a man do but drink?"

"You may well sit there spouting witticisms, you degenerate. You young rich playboys are all alike . . ."

"Now, now, Sir Lionel, walking clichés and all that."

"Fast cars, dance hall girls, and hard drinking. Just a bunch of dangerous ne'er-do-wells, the lot of you. Not letting one of you near my Arabella. Neither of you are fit society for society, if you see what I mean." He drew deeply on his cigar. Fitchly Skorjenhensen glowered at me as he lifted his cue to take his turn.

I looked at Moony, innocuous as a hamster amongst the baize upholstery. I looked at the hulking thug lining up his shot next to the baronet. Something smelled fishy in Sweden, but I couldn't put the finger. Skorjenhensen didn't seem like a natural-born member of the "society" Sir Lionel was referring to. Not that I was bothered by a thing like that—it was 1931 and I for one was feeling pretty progressive. I knew Sir Lionel himself had been born amongst the lower classes, and had built up his business from scratch, as they say, until being raised to the baronetcy after the war. More power to him. Pelham often tells me I don't pay enough attention to class, but I don't pay Pelham to educate me on class issues.

"I look forward to our tennis match tomorrow morning," continued the baronet. "Make fools of you both, I shouldn't be surprised." Fitchly Skorjenhensen chuckled.

I was not to be intimidated. "Bit sinister, what? You've got yourself thinking you're a villain in one of Miss Borogove's novels. I'm looking forward to an invigorating spot of victory myself. Will Mr. Skorjenhensen be able to play off-horse? Perhaps we should try polo?"

Skorjenhensen straightened and trembled. Then he snapped his billiard stick in two. Quite impressive really. Knocked the edge off my bounce, I'll own.

"You don't say a word about my horse," said that worthy. He began moving around the table. Sir Lionel grabbed his jacket.

"Don't," he said. "Not worth insulting our host, even *in absentia*. And look what you've done to your billiard cue."

"He keeps talking about my horse," said Skorjenhensen plaintively. "It makes me angry."

"Put it all in your tennis game tomorrow, you great baby."

32

The big man turned back to the game, muttering darkly as he took a new cue from the rack. "You seem to make my friend here uncomfortable, Mr. Spiffington."

"Damn shame," I said. "He makes me feel warm and fuzzy." This was sarcasm, you understand. I couldn't stand the man. "Perhaps our athletic diversion in the a.m. will serve to break the ice." I put down my empty glass. "Moony, old bean, I feel I may turn in for the evening. Travelling, you know. Woken up at an ungodly hour by the telephone. See you in the morning."

Moony allowed that he was "all in" as well, and got up to join me. As we got to the door, Sir Lionel growled again.

"Look at him, Fitchly! Skulking around after that degenerate like a sheep in a field. Well, we'll give 'em a good shearing in the morning!" And both of the odious things laughed uproariously over the billiard table.

"I hate him, Reggie," said Moony once we'd shut the door. "I truly, truly hate him. What a beastly little man!"

"Cheer up, old chap. Stiff upper whatsit. Think of Arabella and her dreams of your bravery."

"But I *am* thinking of Arabella, Reggie. I'm thinking of how horrible it is that an angel like her should have to live under the thumb of a brute like that."

"Well, she'll hardly be living with him forever. That's part of your plan, isn't it?"

"If he marries her off to that Skorjenhensen, she'll stay under his thumb sure as rain in Sussex. He needs restraint, that one does." You may have picked up on a certain meekness in Moony's character by this point, and it was odd to see him so fierce.

"Moony," I said, "it is odd to see you so fierce. Perhaps a lie down will do you some good."

"Where are you off to?"

"I, my good man, have a night-time picnic to attend."

"Ooo! Can I come? I was rather off my food earlier."

"No, you may not. Ms. Borogove only packed food for two in her lovely little basket."

"Oh. *That* sort of picnic. Oh well. I shall sit disconsolately in the library then."

"Do that, old thing. Best course of action under the circs. I shall return late, but rejuvenated, one hopes, for tomorrow's bit of sport."

And with that I left him.

At eight-fifty that same evening, I walked across the south lawn behind Huffsworthy Hall, past the fountain shaped like the Duke of Wellington, and into the trees. Behind me was Pelham, who was carrying the blanket. We had discussed the events of the evening so far, and Pelham had been good enough to agree that the turn of the tennis plan was a rum thing. Still, he was impressed by Moony and I seemingly having captured the hearts or at least the eyes of the two young women toward whom our own hearts were inclined. As Pelham put it, "Possession is nine-tenths of the law, sir." I had suggested Sir Lionel and Mr. Skorjenhensen were not law-abiding types when it came to this sort of situation, and Pelham had agreed. Soon we came to the clearing of which Mimsy had told me. Impossible, as she said, to miss.

And what an enchanting place it was, too. The trees formed a rough circle twenty yards across or so, leaving a space carpeted with lush grass and one lone oak standing near the center. Lovely spot for a picnic, but I suppose that *was* the point, wasn't it?

"Put the blanket over here, Pelham."

"Yes, sir. If I might suggest turning it at an angle to the tree, sir. Like so." He made a slight adjustment.

"Yes, Pelham, thank you. That's just the thing. Well, it looks quite . . . quite . . ."

"Quite, sir."

"Yes, quite."

"Perhaps it would be prudent for me to withdraw, sir?"

"Oh, crumbs, Pelham, I suppose it would! I'm very fond of you, but perhaps tonight is a solo event, what?"

"I would fervently hope so, sir."

"Very good, Pelham. Have yourself a lovely evening."

"Thank you, sir. I trust you will do the same."

"I plan to, Pelham. I plan to."

Pelham decorously withdrew, leaving me to recline at my leisure on the blanket, and stare at the moon above. My anticipation was at a fever pitch. Mimsy Borogove was quite a woman, and possibly even a match for Reginald Spiffington. The fresh spring air fired my imagination with visions of her green eyes, her flawless white skin, the copper hair which was always slightly disheveled (proper for a bona fide author, I'd say). I went so far as to remove my shoes and socks so I could work my toes into the grass. All thoughts of Moony, Arabella Biscuit, Sir Lionel, and Fitchly Skorjenhensen flitted comfortably out of my brain and ran away into the woods to die of starvation. I may even, dear reader, have hummed a romantic air.

After fifteen minutes I quit humming, but was not demonstrably less chipper. Something must have held the dear girl up. No telling to what sort of conversation she found herself prisoner. I heard what sounded like Sir Lionel shouting somewhere in the distance, perhaps through an open window. I hoped Mimsy was not involved in whatever devilry that man was espousing. Poor dear. I would comfort her once she arrived.

After twenty-five minutes I began to wonder if a chump had been made of me. The rising full moon illuminated the whole area, giving the "lustre of mid-day" to us objects below, as the poem has it. But the night was drawing chill, and I felt the sting of loneliness, I don't mind admitting. Then, about half-past the hour, just as I was beginning to give it up for a loss, I heard someone approaching through the underbrush off to the right. I stood and advanced, barefoot and in my shirt sleeves, to the edge of the trees.

"Ah, at last, my dear one!" I suavely expostulated, "It seems an eternity I have waited, but that's only because moments without you are as years. Why don't you come over to the blanket and we'll GOOD GOD!"

Now would perhaps be an opportune moment to pause and explain that I had at that point in my speech discovered it was not Mimsy Borogove, light of my eyes, approaching through the trees. It was, in fact, a large dog or wolf, which at that moment leapt, teeth bared, snarling for my throat. In light of these circumstances, I think you'll find my choice of language quite appropriate and one might even say restrained.

What ensued might be reasonably called a life or death battle of epic proportions. I had been able to interpose my arm between the thing's jaws and my neck, which I call a small victory, but the weight of it caused me to stagger backward into the clearing and fall face up onto the grass. The brute was huge, and had the full complement of sharp canines and incisors. Neither was the expected accompaniment of slavering and growling neglected. I did my part as well, beating at the beast with my free hand while pushing back across the clearing with my feet and screaming obscenities interspersed with what I hoped were helpful directions to passersby (i.e. "Help, dear God, it's got me" and "I'm being eaten alive").

The moon continued to illuminate the clearing (no idea why it wouldn't, actually, I was just noting), and so I could see the blood from my arm covering my shirt and the wolf's muzzle. I felt myself growing faint; I want to say this was from the weight of the wolf on my chest, which quite drove the air from my lungs, but it is just possible the sight of my own blood was a factor as well. I shan't gainsay it, but would ask how you would have done in the same circs? Now the shoe's on the other foot, eh?

Just as I began to lose consciousness, there came a great thumping blow to the wolf's flank, and the thing yelped and rolled off me. And, faith and glory, what was this? As I blacked out, I could dimly make out the form of Pelham, beating the thing off with an umbrella! I can't express enough the advantages of a good manservant. But I did not even convey my thanks at that particular moment, as I lost consciousness and, as they say, knew no more.

When I came to, I was leaning against the tree. Pelham had bound my arm and was giving me water out of a glass tumbler. My forearm throbbed like anything, and my suit was certainly beyond the pale of my regular cleaner in Bond Street. I felt as if I would swoon again, but Pelham supported my head and spoke to me.

"Ah, very good, sir. I'm happy to see you awake and still with us. You have been injured, not badly, it seems, but in such a way as to cause a greater loss of blood than you perhaps would have wished. Now, I'll need you to stand, and I'll do my best to assist your return to the Hall."

"Where has that horrible beast got to?" I asked. This seemed at the time to be the most pertinent question.

"It appears to be gone, sir. I was able to frighten it away with my umbrella."

"Was it a wolf?"

"It appeared to be, sir."

"Are there wolves in England?"

"Tonight's experience would seem to indicate an affirmative response to that question, sir. Now, can you stand?"

It turned out I could, and with some not inconsiderable help from Pelham, I was able to make it back to the house, through the foyer and into my room. No one else seemed in evidence at that time of night (after ten o'clock), and Pelham went down to the kitchen himself to get warm water and a sponge.

After the arm had been swabbed and wrapped, I sat moodily in my bed, ensconced amongst a sea of pillows and blankets, and provided with a scotch and soda. The night had not turned out in exactly the way I had planned. The main alterations, as I saw it, were Mimsy Borogove not showing up at all for our planned assignation, and having been attacked by a bloody great wolf.

"Perhaps it was a large dog, Pelham?"

"It was most definitely a wolf, sir."

"Mastiff, perhaps?"

"I am afraid not, sir."

"How can you be so irritatingly sure? I could have sworn there were no wolves in England. Didn't my old schoolmaster teach me that in one of my lucid moments during lessons at a tender young age? Hunted to extinction, what?"

"I believe that is the accepted wisdom, sir."

"Then I'm dashed if I know, Pelham. I am, you could accurately say, confounded."

"Your confusion is understandable, sir."

"Perhaps, Pelham, you could enlighten me? Has the animal been imported from Russia? An escapee from a local zoo, I shouldn't wonder? What are your thoughts, Pelham?" For Pelham, as you may have deduced by now, is a fellow who has an inordinate number of thoughts. The man is nearly constantly thinking. The very concept tires me out, but you'd have to get up pretty early to catch my man Pelham not exercising the old bean. And when something as perplexing as having a picnic preempted by an extinct predator occurs, Pelham's just the brain you want in your corner.

"I can't say for certain, sir."

"You mean you have no idea? It is a disturbing conundrum."

"I mean, sir, that the idea which presents itself to me is one which I am loath to share."

I was taken aback. "What do you mean, Pelham? Since when have you not shared ideas with me? There are times, some of them fresh in my memory, when you shared ideas to the point that I fell quite asleep. Share your idea with me."

Pelham sat. This was in itself unusual, and I began to wonder what the deuce was going on. I put it to Pelham in this way: "What the deuce is going on, Pelham?"

"I am afraid, sir, that my information may require a willing suspension of disbelief on your part."

"A willingness to what did you say?"

"An inclination to listen without judgment until I have told all I have to tell."

"Alright, Pelham, old boy. I have to say, you've become highly atypical this evening."

"Yes, sir. My apologies, sir."

"Oh, no apologies necessary, Pelham. The whole evening has been the least typical I could have imagined. Tell on, my good man, I am not going anywhere."

"I believe you were attacked by something that was in fact a wolf, but which may in fact be something else as well."

"I'm not sure I'm following you. My disbelief is suspended to the ceiling—it's not that, you see—but it's a wolf and yet something else as well. Some sort of wolf-dog hybrid, perhaps?"

"No, sir. I believe," and here he paused like an actor in a radio drama, "that you were attacked by a werewolf."

"I say, Pelham, are you feeling alright?"

"Yes, sir. I am most well. I am being completely serious when I say—"

"Because when you said 'werewolf' just then I had a clear thought. 'Reggie,' said my thought, 'Pelham's going round the pipe.' I don't often have thoughts, Pelham, and I find it neighborly to agree with them when they do occur."

"If you would be so kind, sir, as to let me finish."

"Certainly, Pelham. Rant away, my good lunatic."

"Thank you, sir. Before I worked for you, I was employed by a man named Coverdale. Mr. Coverdale was a member of an organization that spent its time dabbling in the dark arts."

"What, like macramé?"

"No, sir. Though Mr. Coverdale was not unfamiliar with the craft of macramé, I do not mean that. I mean that these men, and women, attempted to influence people and events through the use of magic."

"Ah, I see. Houdini, what?"

"More on the order of Aleister Crowley, sir."

"Oh, I see. I say, Pelham, that's a bit sinister, isn't it?"

"Yes, sir. It was owing to the, as you say, sinister nature of Mr. Coverdale's magical endeavors that I eventually left his employ. I am much more comfortable working for someone like yourself, sir."

"Thank you, Pelham."

"Not at all, sir. While I was still serving as butler to Mr. Coverdale, I became privy to information about the world we live in that can be considered disturbing. I learned of these things occasionally directly from my employer, but more often from the servants of other members of his order."

"What was the name of that order, Pelham?"

"The Order of the Jaunty Pomegranate, a name drawn from Greek myth, I believe. It was through the testimony of these other servants, mostly from one in particular, that I came to know the truth of certain peasant superstitions which seem to most of the world the stuff of Gothic novels."

"You mean, like werewolves? Reynolds' Wagner, Parisian alleyways, all that?"

"I'm not conversant with the reference, sir, but I do mean, among other things, werewolves—people who become wolves when the moon is full."

"And you think that the beast that attacked me was one of those."

"Yes, sir."

"And upon what criteria do you make such a classification, Pelham? The thing was no doubt wearing a double-breasted waistcoat and a pocket-watch?"

"I cannot find humor in the situation, sir. I base my conjecture, and I will admit that it is only conjecture, on three pieces of evidence. One is the size of the creature that attacked you. It was much larger than any naturally occurring wolf of which I am aware. Certainly larger than the wolves in London Zoo. Secondly, the fullness of the moon. And finally, the fact that, as you've said, there are no wolves in the wild in England."

"I see. Do you know, this is the most I've ever heard you reveal about your past, Pelham? And I wish you hadn't."

"I am sorry, sir. But I felt it important to convey my suspicions to you in light of what has happened."

"In light of . . . ? I'm afraid once again I am at a loss, Pelham."

"I beg your pardon, sir. I should have been more explicit. You have been bitten by a werewolf. If the stories are to be believed, you will become a wolf tomorrow evening."

Chapter Four

I slept well that evening, despite Pelham's abysmal bedtime story. Apparently, according to my suddenly knowledgeable and mysterious manservant, werewolves transform on three nights of the month: before, during, and after the full moon. Though the moon had looked full to me in the clearing where I had been savaged, it was actually just at the end of its waxing. Tonight would be the real thing, followed by Sunday night's beginning of the wane, so to speak. I had a scant eighteen hours or so before the supernatural change came upon me, by Pelham's calculations. But these things troubled me not a jot as I slumbered like a babe amongst the eiderdown.

In the light of the morning sun I found the events of the previous evening somewhat more difficult to credit, which is to say the whole thing seemed like a load of codswallop, if I have properly used that colorful colloquialism. The animal that had leaped at me was almost certainly a large dog, and the full moon was a coincidence that couldn't be helped. You can't expect the moon to bypass its appointed rounds simply because a wild dog is loose in the woods. Pelham had obviously been exposed to some dangerous ideas by his former employer which had made him susceptible to wild flights of fancy in the moonlight, traces of which tendency were not to be seen during his normal day to day existence. Poor man.

More pressing for me was the question of Mimsy Borogove. Where had she got off to the night before? I intended to have a word or two with that lovely little stand-up artist. As I dressed, I found that my arm wasn't injured nearly as badly as it had seemed the night before. In fact, the thing was nearly good as new. Everything had seemed worse during the night, apparently. I called for Pelham and had him ready the togs whilst I lathered and brushed.

"How is your arm this morning, sir?"

"As right as rain, Pelham my good man. Or as near as next door." I waggled my fingers to demonstrate. Nothing like a good finger waggle to show your arm is on the up and up. "Not as bad as we thought, eh, Pelham?"

"The injury was a nasty one, sir, though not particularly deep. Your rapid healing would seem further proof of my hypothesis of last evening."

"Yes, well, perhaps Spiffington stock is healthier than most. I must admit, Pelham, you had me going with your wild tales last night. It was most diverting; I am most appreciative."

"Sir. I feel compelled to once again express my strongest—"

"I have not the slightest doubt that you do, Pelham. But I must away. I smell the unmistakable odor of fresh bacon. I am here primarily to sup from the pot of Dobbins, and my nose tells me that his pot is now astir. Fare thee well, Pelham. I'll see you after I have breakfasted."

And away I went. The breakfast room was rather crowded, and the crowd was rather interesting in several disparate ways. First off, our host had returned from London and was seated at the head of the table, fresh from the road and still dressed in his driving coat. He grimaced when he saw me, but had the decency to nod and to take my proffered hand whilst I murmured the requisite "Lord Huffsworthy, it's been much too long."

Sir Lionel was there, as was his bulky toady Fitchly Skorjenhensen. The former was still round and effusively offensive, but the great Swede had encountered some sort of further accident during the night. The fine tracery of scars I had happily attributed to yesterday's briar patch had been amended with a large bruise across the right side of his face and a sharp cut underneath the eye. He looked sulkier than usual, which is a feat worthy of praise. Moony was just coming in as I arrived and was seating himself to the left of Arabella Biscuit, who wore a shapeless pale yellow dress and had dark circles under her eyes. Mimsy was there already, looking somewhat disheveled, and she smiled sheepishly at me as I took my seat. She could not, of course, offer explanation or beg forgiveness among so many, but her coppery curls were enough to soften me until I recalled the full extent of my inconvenience the night before. I gave her a disapproving tut and looked expectantly for the eggs and rashers. Signor Reynaldo MacGregor was also present.

"What the devil," said Sir Lionel, "happened to you?" He was looking at the bandaged arm which I had propped amongst the butter dishes. "Some sort of ruse to escape being trounced at tennis this morning?" He chuckled. The man was always chuckling; a veritable chuckling franchise was he.

"Just a little scratch. I'm fit as a fiddle. I'm a little worried about your man Skorjenhensen, though. He looks like he's been drug through the woods by his horse."

The big Swede looked up startled. "My horse would never—"

"However did you come by that shiner, my good man? Looks like you've been whacked by a great stick."

"Tripped over the edging on the gravel path, didn't I?"

"That's got to sting. If you'd rather not run around the court this morning, I'm sure we'd all understand."

"Oh, Fitchly will be fine," said Sir Lionel. "It's sure to be decidedly unstrenuous."

"How was London, Lord Huffsworthy?" asked Mimsy in a thinly veiled attempt to intervene.

Lord Huffsworthy was a thin, doleful man who was mostly mustache. He looked at Mimsy as if she had just told him he had a terminal illness. "London was London," he said. "It neither shrinks nor grows. New and bigger things appear every time I am there, and yet there is never any real change. Surely you've been?"

"Oh, yes, I live in London," said Mimsy, "in Bayswater."

"Then you know how London was," said Lord Huffsworthy. I had finished my porridge and was eagerly awaiting the next course. "I was expecting bacon to be here already," I said to Moony. "I smelled it while I was dressing."

"You must have an extraordinary sense of smell," said Lord Huffsworthy in a sepulchral voice. "I was just told by Bugsby that Dobbins has only just now begun the bacon. It should be here momentarily, with the fruit."

"Nose of a dog," said Fitchly Skorjenhensen distinctly. "Matches the rest of his bloody face."

I dropped my spoon. "I mean to say! Lord Huffsworthy! What sorts of guests do you allow to spend the weekend at your Hall? This man has done nothing but insult me since I arrived!"

There followed an odd and awkward pause. I would like to say my small outburst had caused embarrassment on the part of my tormentors and their host, if only for the sheer joy of righteous indignation vindicated. But that didn't seem to be the case. Sir Lionel and Fitchly Skorjenhensen exchanged looks which I'm dashed if I can describe with any word other than "sinister." Unless perhaps I used the word "knowing" or "dastardly." Truth be told, I can actually think of dozens of words to describe it, but all of them carry a negative connotation. And while these two exchanged their multi-adjectived yet mostly sinister look, Lord Huffsworthy looked more doleful than ever. I saw Mimsy notice. Moony and Arabella noticed nothing but Moony and Arabella. Signor MacGregor had gotten porridge on his cuffs. Lord Huffsworthy had certainly heard me, but he did not respond. The bacon and eggs arrived, with more coffee and blueberries with cream.

"At any rate," said Mimsy into the silence, "the food is smashing. It doesn't matter in what order it's served. Dobbins is a wonder!"

"Oh, yes," answered Sir Lionel. "He always has been. I've always wanted a chef like Dobbins for Biscuit Manor. And I'm happy to say the likelihood increases daily."

Lord Huffsworthy dropped his spoon. He looked on the verge of tears. This isn't unusual for Lord Huffsworthy, but this morning it appeared the old ducts might actually begin to produce. Sir Lionel gave another of his knowing glances, which surely must have a patent pending in some government facial registry.

"What's going on?" Mimsy asked. The atmosphere had become too odd not to comment. Once again it was that odious little baronet who answered her.

"Our host wonders how he would get on without a great chef in the house," he said.

"Well, surely that's not an issue," said Moony, who had finally noticed things were souring to the point that two spoons had been dropped. "Dobbins has been with us for years. Very happy and all that."

"Yes, we're all very happy aren't we?" said the baronet, laughing inexplicably.

Fitchly Skorjenhensen also found humor in the statement, apparently. "Oh yes," he mimicked, "very happy." Sir Lionel shot a look at him, and I got the distinct impression all was not sweetmeats and moonbeams in Biscuit-land. Fitchly looked back at his food rather than meet Sir Lionel's gaze.

Lord Huffsworthy visibly saddened, something of which only he is capable, and stood. "If you will excuse me for a moment," he said, and stepped nimbly from the room.

"Father?" said Moony, and followed him. Arabella watched him go, a look of longing in her vague little eyes, but then she caught sight of Fitchly Skorjenhensen looking at her, and she blushed to the roots of her hair, before looking back at her plate.

Mimsy looked as if she would follow, but Sir Lionel, constant source of breakfast conversation, spoke again. "Oh, don't bother. *He'll* be all right. Bloody great boob of a man with a bloody great boob of a son. Breakfast will be pleasanter without 'em."

Once again, my dander had risen. I'm not usually an angry young man, and on most days, even in trying circumstances, you'll find my dander right down there where etiquette dictates, but this man, I mean to say. "What the devil do you mean by it?" I queried. "The man is your host! What sort of way is that to talk about the owner of the house to which you've been invited and in which you are enjoying a comfortable weekend? And whether you have seen it or not, that 'great booby of a son' as you call him is in love with your daughter." I turned to Arabella. "And if I may be so bold, Miss Biscuit, you seem to be in love with him!" Arabella turned a brilliant shade of scarlet and hid behind her toast.

"Egad," said Sir Lionel, "the things you don't know! My connection with Lord Huffsworthy is based on conditions that will always find me welcome in this house, whether he wants it that way or not. I'm not under any obligations, you might say. And as for that bloody baby of a son," and here he looked at Arabella, "there are no circumstances possible under which I'd allow that dripping milksop anywhere near my daughter. She is a delicate creature and will be saved for someone who can take care of her."

Here Arabella actually came somewhat to life. "Daddy! You don't know Moony! He's perfectly able to take care of me. He's wealthy, and sweet, and kind, and—"

"And a bloody great baby!" roared her father. By now everyone but Fitchly Skorjenhensen had abandoned the pretext of breakfast. Arabella stood up and fled the room in tears.

"Now look what you've done!" said Sir Lionel, rising. "She's upset by your ridiculous claptrap. Go after her Fitchly; she'll need your comforting."

The huge Swede looked up, bacon between his lips. "But I'm still having my ruddy breakfast!"

"Go!" barked Sir Lionel. The big man laid down his fork and knife, stood up, and went. Sir Lionel eyed Mimsy and I with a beady squint. "A bloody woman writer and a bloody useless playboy! And you have the gall to ask Lord Huffsworthy what sort of guests he lets stay here. Makes me sick to my stomach!" And, seizing a rasher of bacon and downing his glass of pineapple juice, Sir Lionel Biscuit, bart., waddled from the room.

"What do you make of all that?" asked Mimsy Borogove as I tucked into my eggs.

"Hideous people," I said. "Nary a drop of couth between them."

"What is going on between Sir Lionel and Lord Huffsworthy, do you think?"

"Hmm? I'm sure I don't know. Beyond his Lordship being disgusted by the man's behavior. Made him sadder than usual, if that's possible. What do you mean?" I speared a mouthful of egg.

"Surely you noticed the meaningful looks and the odd comments about 'not being under any obligations.' Something is definitely up." She looked shrewdly toward the door. Mimsy's shrewd look was quite fetching. Crinkled nose, bit of stray hair. In fact, the most aesthetically pleasing specimen of shrewdness I ever had the pleasure to see.

"They do seem rather unconventional companions," I said.

"You think the baronet has some hold over Lord Huffsworthy?" She continued fetchingly. "I don't know yet," she admitted. "Dobbins alluded to some strange goings-on when I spoke with him last night. It's very odd, Reggie."

"My evening was surprisingly odd in itself," I said, segueing so smoothly I'm surprised she noticed. "Got bitten by a dog. Can't imagine what I was doing out in the woods."

"Oh, Reggie, you must let me explain," began Mimsy.

"In the night, the wolf, it howls," said Signor MacGregor, whom we had both forgotten.

"What did you say?" I asked. "Did you mention a wolf? There aren't any wolves in England, my good man."

"Thatsa may be," said the tenor, "but itsa howl just the same." He went back to his toast.

Mimsy and I left the breakfast room, she going up the stairs to her room before I could rekindle the conversation. I wandered toward the library, hoping to find a Huffsworthy of some kind. Instead I found Pelham and Arabella Biscuit. Pelham was standing beside the leather armchair on which Arabella sat drying her eyes and looking up at him.

"Ah, Mr. Spiffington," said Pelham upon my entrance, "you are perhaps just the person necessary. Miss Biscuit has been telling me a most heartbreaking story, which perhaps you should be privy to."

"Miss Biscuit was . . . why, Pelham, you've never struck me as a feminine confidant!"

"My talents, sir, are varied and deep. I have little opportunity to be the confidant of the fairer sex since entering your employ, though I *have* received confidential communications from several young women of your acquaintance upon termination of the relationship."

"You've received what did you say?"

"The matter at hand, sir, is Miss Biscuit's distress." He

turned back to the Noodle. "Miss Biscuit," he said, "perhaps you could share with Mr. Spiffington what you have been telling me."

Arabella Biscuit looked at me with her watery eyes. Her crying had increased their moisture to the extent I feared her corneas would drown. "My father is a very bad man, Mr. Spiffington," she said. "I am afraid he doesn't have good intentions for the Huffsworthys."

"Well, I shan't gainsay those two statements, my dear. I hardly thought he was planning a surprise party for Moony."

"No, I mean he has specific bad intentions. Lord Huffsworthy knows why my father has come, and that's why he was so upset at the breakfast table."

This was certainly scoring higher and higher on the oddness scale. "Why is he here?" I asked.

"He's come to claim a debt. Lord Huffsworthy was foolish enough to—"

"Ah, there you are, my Light of Life!" expostulated Moony as he entered. "I've been looking for you ever since I left Father. He's ever so glum and I can't for the life of me figure it out."

Arabella closed her mouth and smiled, clearly off the subject and unwilling to get back on. She stood and took Moony's hands as he approached her and kissed her pale cheek. "My darling!" he said. Arabella leaned forward to meet Moony's quivering lips, and as she did the collar of her dress slipped down and revealed a series of nasty bruises along the nape of her neck. I heard Pelham's sharp intake of breath as I involuntarily said, "Good lord!"

Arabella Biscuit drew back quickly from Moony and pulled her collar higher. She looked at the floor, embarrassed. Moony saw the direction of our concerned gazes and reached up to pull the collar back down. The bruises were gray and yellow, with newer, bluish-black ones overlaced. Moony was reasonably shocked.

"Arabella! What is this? My god, darling, what has happened to you?"

Arabella Biscuit continued looking at the floor, a pale blush spreading over her neck and face. She did not answer.

"Miss Biscuit," said Pelham, in the kindest voice I'd ever

heard him use. "Mr. Huffsworthy is concerned for your welfare. If I might be so bold, I must confess to sharing his concern."

"Me, too," I put in, not about to be outcompassioned. "I'm concerned as all get-out!"

"Indeed, we all have a natural wish to know how you came by the injuries which are plainly visible here."

"Arabella," said Moony softly, "did . . . did your father do this?"

Arabella pulled her head up sharply and looked at Moony, tears in her eyes. "He is," she said, "a very bad man." And she ran from the room. It was quite the morning for running from rooms.

Moony watched her go. The look in his eyes was so fierce I had trouble believing it was the same old Moony. "That rotter," he said. "That absolute, utter rotter."

"Moony, I don't know what to say. I would never have guessed it, even of Sir Lionel."

"He's evil," said Moony. "He's done something to devastate the old man, and now this . . . this . . . well. There's nothing for it, then." Moony smiled at me and then calmly walked from the room, ignoring my requests he not do anything rash.

"I say, Pelham. I mean, dash it."

"Indeed, sir. I find the situation most disturbing."

"What was Arabella going to tell me?"

"I am afraid I don't know, sir. She had gotten to the same point when you came in. In asking her to tell you, I expected to hear the complete story for the first time."

"Well, Pelham, I mean to say. Dash it."

"So you've said, sir. Perhaps you should follow Mr. Huffsworthy to ensure nothing untoward happens."

"Good man, Pelham. That's just the thing."

"And, sir?"

"Yes, Pelham?"

"I have been thinking about our conversation after the events of last night."

"Ah, well, Pelham, that's okay. We all make asses of ourselves—"

"And it occurs to me the werewolf must be an inhabitant of

this house. Either one of the owners or servants regularly resident here, or else one of the guests."

"Yes, well, we can go shopping for straight-jackets when we return to London. I think at this point I should follow Moony."

"I merely suggest you keep your eyes open, sir."

"I'll do that, Pelham."

I went looking for Moony. This supernatural bent of Pelham's was a rum thing. I had no intention of telling him of Signor MacGregor's strange outburst at the breakfast table, and hoped the topic would die out. My arm felt good as new, and as I left the library I pulled the bandage loose and dropped it in a wastepaper basket in the hallway. I was moving towards the drawing room in hopes of finding Moony, when Mimsy came rushing down the stairs and pulled me to the side near the door to the smoking room.

"Reggie, darling," she said breathlessly, "it's gone!"

"I'm sorry to hear it, Mimsy old girl, but that's a rather vague beginning, isn't it?"

"My manuscript, Reggie! It's gone. It was in the desk in my room, and now it's gone. Come up and see!"

I'll admit I had hoped to be invited to Mimsy Borogove's room at some point during the weekend, but I'll be frank that this didn't seem the time or the circumstances calculated to make me dance a jig in response. And yet, anything I could do for Mimsy . . .

"I was just after Moony right now, but I suppose a quick look 'round wouldn't hurt. Do you think it might have slipped under the dresser or something?"

She pulled me by the hand and we started up the stairs. "One hundred and fifty-seven pages of type-written high-quality bond paper does not 'slip under the dresser' Reggie!" she said.

"Oh I don't know. I once found the L-O volume of the Encyclopedia Britannica wedged underneath a claw-foot bathtub in grandfather's summer house. Its presence was a perfect conundrum until I recalled an episode months before when I was in the bath and couldn't remember the proper ratio of rum to butter in a traditional Hot Toddy. So what happened was that I—"

"Here it is," said Mimsy. We had arrived in her boudoir, site of many an imagined romantic rendezvous in the Spiffington diary. She was pointing to the desk, the center drawer of which was standing half-open. I'm no expert in analyzing a crime scene, but what with the twisted lock and the heavily scratched mahogany, I feel fairly safe in declaring the locked drawer forced.

"Good lord, Mimsy! Who would steal a half-written manuscript? I mean, I know your novels are worth money, but not until they're finished, I wouldn't imagine."

"Oh, I know exactly who did this. Sir Lionel Biscuit did this!"

"Come now, Mimsy. Why would the baronet steal your manuscript? He's a horrible little man, even worse than I'd guessed, I'm finding, but that hardly seems like something that would interest him."

"What do you mean, worse than you'd guessed?"

I told her what we had discovered about Sir Lionel's treatment of his daughter moments ago in the library. "That's where I was going when you found me—to catch Moony."

"My God, what humans are capable of," said Mimsy, shaking her lovely head. "That poor girl. But that's only the more reason to stop the man. He stole my manuscript because he knows what it's about."

"*Murder by Bratwurst*? It's about culinary crime, isn't it? That's what all your books are about."

"Yes, but this one is about the murder of a horrible little man who has been milking his wealthy friends for all they're worth."

"I don't follow you."

"That's what I was trying to talk to you about in the breakfast room earlier, you goose. Why do you think Sir Lionel is here?"

I was beginning to weary of this line of talk. "I'll be jiggered if I know, Mimsy my dear. People keep asking me that question, but no one will answer it!"

"Lord Huffsworthy is in debt to Sir Lionel. You must know that Sir Lionel was not a born member of the aristocracy. He got his title through the same means as he's used to pin old Huffsworthy to the wall."

"You mean he's a swindler of some sort?"

"He's a glorified loan shark, as they call it in the American gangster films. He loans money at exorbitant interest. Takes all manner of collateral as well. An all-around bad man, and he's got Lord Huffsworthy over a barrel, from what I can tell."

"How do you know this?"

"Dobbins told me. I was the first guest to arrive yesterday afternoon, and I spent some time talking to Dobbins in the kitchen. You learn the most amazing things from servants. He wasn't sure of the details, but he knew why Sir Lionel was coming. Lord Huffsworthy had apparently gone to London on Thursday to try and scare up the funds somehow. Based on his actions at breakfast I'd say he was unsuccessful."

"And you're writing a book about it?"

"Well, I've based a character on Sir Lionel, which isn't quite the same thing. And I made the mistake of telling him."

"That was a rum call!"

"I didn't come out and say 'hey there you loan shark, I've put you in a book!' But I did say enough about the character that a thinking man could have put two and two together. Or even Sir Lionel. I had the character as a sort of generic bad person. It wasn't until talking with Dobbins that I went back last night and added the details about loans and extortion. But I mentioned my intentions in the drawing room before you arrived."

"And Sir Lionel remarked it?"

"He said something on the order of 'bloody women writers' and 'slander is a common word in the courts' and 'useless bloody waste of time, detective novels.' So of course I delighted in making my villain as Sir Lionel-like as possible. Took me most of the night."

"Did it?"

"Yes, it did. That's one reason I want that manuscript back so badly. I've put in a fair amount of work on that one."

"It's funny, you know, I had expected a picnic in the woods last night. Got rather excited about it. Could have caught pneumonia, if I hadn't been driven inside by a rabid dog."

"Oh, Reggie! I'm so so sorry, darling! That's what I was going to tell you at breakfast when that odd little Signor MacGregor interrupted. I sat down after dinner to put down a page or two, and found myself so caught up in the story that by the time I got my head about me it was after eleven. I feel such a heel."

"Confound it, Mimsy; I was sitting in the bloody grass for forty-five minutes. And then I was starring in a particularly violent production of Little Red Riding Hood. Not a pleasant evening, Mimsy. And my hopes, I must tell you, were high."

"Oh, my poor poor darling. You will let me make it up to you, won't you?" And here Mimsy Borogove played rough. She stretched up and kissed my cheek. Dastardly tactic, that. Game, set, and match for her.

"I'm sure we can find some way to correct the oversight," I said.

"Oh, good, darling. I was just as disappointed as you, you know. For now, though," and she became business-like again, "we've got to find my manuscript. What time were you supposed to play tennis with Sir Lionel?"

"Oh, crumbs! In all this melodrama I had quite forgotten. I think we had agreed on ten o'clock. I'm not sure Moony will be in the state of mind to play against the man, after what he's done to Arabella."

"What time is it now?"

I looked at my watch. "Dash it all, it's ten minutes to."

So we went down. Mimsy said she would meet me outside, so I sauntered out alone to the side garden. Fitchly Skorjenhensen was on the court, in a pair of cotton pants made for someone a quarter smaller than he. He wore a straw boater that looked as if it wished he hadn't. The sunlight showed plainly the scars and bruises on Skorjenhensen's face. Neither Moony nor Sir Lionel were in evidence, and neither was anyone else, except Reynaldo MacGregor, who was sitting in a lawn chair by the side of the court waiting patiently for the game to begin.

"Where are our partners?" I asked the huge man.

"Tain't seen 'em," he said. "I thought they'd have been here by now. Ain't the little fellow with you?"

"Well, he hardly seems to be, does he? I didn't know you went places that Sir Lionel didn't."

"Ach," he expectorated, "Sir Lionel. Little blighter's getting too cheeky for his own good. Barking orders at me like I was a common kitchen-boy. And that daughter of his!" He shook his big blond block of a head.

"You have decided Arabella is not the girl for you? Fresher fish in the seas, what?"

"Don't you say a word against Arabella Biscuit! She's a fine, fine girl, is Arabella. She's a right peach, she is. But she's no wife of mine."

"But I thought he wanted the two of you together?"

"Who bleeding knows," he returned, bouncing a tennis ball with his racquet. "But he don't always get what he wants, alright?"

"All right. But that's fairly mutinous talk, my friend. Sir Lionel doesn't seem like a man to be crossed."

"You can tell him whatever I say. I'm nearly through with that one. And if you do tell him, I'll say you're lying and thump you on the head, really hard."

"Well, there's that," I admitted. "Tip-top argument, actually."

"After last night, I'm nearly done, I am."

"Why?" I asked, "what happened last night?"

"I was supposed to follow you wherever you went, right?"

"What? That's the first I've heard of that."

Skorjenhensen looked at me like I was thick. "Well, of course you didn't know. What good would it be to follow you wherever you went, if you knew I was following you? Anyway, after what I saw in the woods, I don't know how he expects me to—"

But I never heard what Sir Lionel expected Fitchly Skorjenhensen to do. We were interrupted then by a scream from the house. We both sprinted into the foyer, where we were met by the downstairs maid, Jane, who was on her way out. She gestured hysterically toward the drawing room, and ran out the door. I don't put myself forward as an astute observer of human behavior, but it seemed to me at that point exploring the drawing room might provide a clue to the maid's actions, and so I crossed the hall and entered the drawing room.

The room was occupied by Sir Lionel Biscuit, bart., who was lying face-down on the fur rug next to the table with the scotch on it. He was dead.

Chapter Five

It was over two hours before the doctor arrived from the neighboring village of Huffton-On-Spry, but the police were there within thirty minutes. Which is as it should be, really. The police had work to do, and one look at Sir Lionel laying there on the rug was enough to tell even the dimmest bulb that a doctor was among the list of superfluous items for the former baronet. He lay—sprawled is the correct term—across the center of the rug, his left hand reaching out toward the fireplace. His fingers were curled into horrible contortions, and his face was frozen into a grimace utterly unlike the grimace he wore naturally. There was an unbecoming froth at his lips, and an overturned chair near his feet. His foul cigar still smoldered in an ashtray next to the scotch bottle. The body—corpse? carcass?—was still warm as I checked for a pulse.

The maid's screams had brought the rest of the house to see what the commotion was, and I had to move quickly to prevent Arabella from entering the room along with Moony, Mimsy, Lord Huffsworthy, and the servants. I blocked the door and whispered to Moony that he should keep Miss Biscuit occupied in the library while we determined what to do.

The rest of us stood in a semi-circle around the late Sir Lionel, wondering how to proceed and, I expect, thinking all

around that a show of grief might be called for but finding ourselves unable to call for it at present. I could detect a faint odor
of flower, or something gardeny, underneath the cigar stench, as
well as a trace of perfume in the air. Olfactory prowess probably
in the genes. While we were standing there the police arrived,
called, I assumed, by a member of the staff.

Chief Inspector Pail and Detective Inspector Mutton were
all business as they entered the house, which is to say they ushered everyone into the library and refused to talk to anyone until
they had seen the body. We waited quietly while they did whatever it is the police do when confronted with a dead baronet.
Arabella Biscuit had been informed of her father's death, and
was taking it admirably well. All of us were subdued, naturally,
by the presence of death among us. The strangest reaction out
of the gate was that of Fitchly Skorjenhensen, who was sobbing
like a child in the corner. For someone who was just telling me
how he was "nearly done" with Sir Lionel, he took the loss hard.
Moony was grim-faced and doting, bringing Arabella whatever
she needed and in general being the lovestruck chap in a crisis.
Mimsy Borogove stood by one of the tall windows between the
shelves and fidgeted with the curtains. Lord Huffsworthy looked
doleful, but also thoughtful, and I wondered if his thoughts were
turning on the debt Sir Lionel came to extract from him. Signor
MacGregor was there as well.

As for myself, the whole thing seemed so odd I couldn't credit
it. I had just spoken with the ill-tempered little man at breakfast,
not an hour and a half before. I remembered it distinctly: the
blighter had called me a useless playboy. I couldn't say I'd spend
time missing the man. I wandered over to Mimsy.

"Well, what do you make of all this?" I asked in an undertone.

"I think he was an unloved troll. And I'm wondering if they'll
find my manuscript on his body."

"I say, that's rather harsh, isn't it? None of us got on with the
man but, I mean to say."

"Are you cut up over his death?"

"Well, no, I can't say as I am."

"Is there anyone here who is? I mean, perhaps Arabella is
momentarily saddened, but won't her life be better? Bloody

woman-beater! I suppose that hulking blonde chap may miss him."

"Actually, he was just telling me he was done with Sir Lionel. Something about seeing something in the woods last night."

"What did he see?"

"Haven't the faintest. The grim hand of the Reaper intervened in our discussion."

"Who do you think did it?" Mimsy asked, looking over her shoulder at the other inhabitants of the room.

"Did what?"

"Don't be obtuse, Reggie darling. Who do you think did the nasty little man in?"

"What? Who said he was murdered?"

"Obviously he was murdered. He was universally hated, he seemed hale and hearty. He wandered out of the breakfast room fit as a fiddle and an hour later we find him dead in the drawing room. Someone killed him."

"I don't know he was fit as a fiddle. For all I know he had a weak heart, or angina, or coronary issues. He may have been a walking death-trap. You've been writing too many murder mysteries."

"Perhaps. Name someone here who isn't better off without him."

"Pelham. In point of fact, Pelham's brain will be of assistance here." I motioned to Pelham, who joined us at the window. It was getting rather crowded at the window now, but we could persevere as long as no one else decided to take in the air. "Pelham," I said, "Mimsy feels Sir Lionel has been the victim of foul play."

"Yes, sir. That much seems obvious."

"Why? It's not obvious to me."

"Sir Lionel Biscuit gave every appearance of being healthy and fit. He was strongly disliked by everyone in the house, including the servants. He was assumedly fine at breakfast, and an hour later we find him expired on the drawing room rug."

"Oh, Mimsy, stop making that sort of face."

"If you think of it, sir," continued Pelham, "nearly everyone in this room is in a better situation with Sir Lionel gone."

"Look, did you two plan this out ahead of time?"

"We're just assessing the facts, Reggie," said Mimsy, patting my face.

At that point Pail and Mutton came into the library. Mutton moved about the room looking at each person therein while making notes in a small moleskine notebook. Pail stood in front of the door with his hands behind his back for a minute and a half, until he was sure everyone was looking at him. He was not what most people would call easy to look at, and by most people I refer mainly to the sighted. He gave one the suggestion of a Sunday roast that had put on a uniform and grown a moustache. As we awaited his utterance, he held up a single finger in front of his face like a warning.

"There has been a murder committed here," said Chief Inspector Pail. Mimsy and Pelham both murmured, "Mmm-hmm." I gave them a cold glance. The Inspector continued, "Now, is there anyone else about the premises besides those gathered here?"

It turns out there was. Dobbins was still in the kitchen, and Sir Lionel's own manservant Smythe was upstairs in Sir Lionel's room reading the racing papers. They were brought into the room with us. While Mutton looked them over and made more notes, Pail went on.

"Now, here we all are. Yes, I feel confident we have all been brought together." No one gainsaid him. "Now, here's the thing, see. We can't have any of you lot going off and getting yourselves unfindable, if you follow my drift. I'm afraid I'm going to have to request that no one leave the premises until we have concluded our investigation of this tragic incident."

"Now look here," said Lord Huffsworthy, who looked less doleful than he had at breakfast. "These people, besides my son and the servants, are here as my guests. I can't have you people incommoding them." He looked very much the country squire.

"Ah, but Lord Huffsworthy," said Pail, once again holding up his formidable finger. "Sir Lionel was also your 'guest,' wasn't he? And one of these good folk in the room have gone and killed him!"

We all looked at each other. It followed, of course. And Mimsy had suggested as much moments before. But now the thought that one of us was a cold-blooded killer seemed so very what-do-you-mean that I had to suppress a shudder.

"Now, if you all will just stay put, we'll see what we can see."

"Are we required to remain in this room?" asked Lord Huffsworthy.

"No, your lordship, I can't see as there's a reason for all that. But I can't be having anyone leave the premises."

"Of course," said Lord Huffsworthy. "We shall all of course comply with your investigation."

"Chief Inspector," said Mimsy, "could you tell us how Sir Lionel died?"

Pail turned his attention to her. "Ah, is that Miss Mimsy Borogove? I am indeed honored to meet you, Miss Borogove. I recognize you from your photograph on your book jackets. I simply loved *Just Desserts*. What a clever, clever woman you must be."

"I appreciate your saying so. How did Sir Lionel die?"

"I can't say, Miss Borogove. The doctor is examining the body now, and it'll take a full coroner's report before we can say something like that."

"Does it appear to be some sort of poison?"

"Now, now, Miss Borogove. This is no murder mystery novel, this here. What we have here is a bona fide murder, and while you are among the best I've ever seen at fictional crime, this is, if you'll forgive me, the real thing. I'm afraid I'll have to ask you to leave it to the professionals. Now if you'll all excuse me." He roasted from the room.

"He thinks I did it," said Mimsy.

"No, no. Why would he think you did it?"

"I know how these things work, Reggie. I write about them. I know about people getting killed. I didn't like Sir Lionel, and I accused him of stealing my manuscript."

"Not to his face. You only told me you thought he had taken your manuscript. And now, of course, you've told everyone in the room."

"Oi, why do you think Lionel took your ruddy book?" This from our Swede.

"I don't mean to discuss this matter with you, Mr. Skorjenhensen," said Mimsy stiffly.

"And why did you ask just now about poison? What do you know about this, Miss Borogove?" Everyone was looking at Mimsy now. I put a protective arm around her, taking charge of the situation and all that. She roughly pushed it off.

"Because there appeared to be no other obvious cause of death. He didn't seem to be wounded. There was no visible bruising on the face and head. It stands to reason that—"

"Bloody suspicious if you ask me."

I stepped in front of Fitchly Skorjenhensen. "Well, where were you?"

"What? I was with you on the bloody tennis court out-bloody-side!"

"You were there five minutes before the body was found, but what about during the hour or so after breakfast?"

"I was with Sir Lionel for a while, and then I went up to . . . look, I don't have to explain myself to you, you little worm! Where were you?"

"I was talking with Moony and Arabella, and then I was with Mimsy. I think that you—"

But I was interrupted by Lord Huffsworthy, who spoke in a sadly authoritative voice. "Where were any of us?" We all turned to look at his Lordship. "Is there any one of us that has an iron-clad alibi for every moment between leaving the breakfast table and the finding of the body? Most of us had a disagreement with Sir Lionel or else disliked him. Your pardon, Miss Biscuit, but I speak what is surely the truth. We are all suspects, except for Sir Lionel himself, who is dead."

Lord Huffsworthy knows how to enliven a party. But I suppose if his intention was to inject a little reality into the proceedings, then job well done. Bravo, your Lordship. Suitably chastened, we scattered.

We didn't scatter far. Policemen were posted at every door like stone Chinamen, and the place was crawling with detectives and coroners and white coats and blue coats and I don't know who all. Rather impressive coordination of efforts, for a bloated little rubbish heap like Sir Lionel Biscuit, but that's the sub-peerage for you. As most of the public spaces in the house were infested with investigators of some stripe or other, I imitated most of the other guests and went to my room, where I tried to read a five-year-old copy of *Punch* while Pelham ironed various pieces of my clothing. I was not usually in during the day, and between the bustle of Pelham and the thought of the dead man downstairs, I found it difficult to focus on the witticisms in the Punchian pages. I resorted to conversation.

"What do you make of it all, Pelham?"

"You refer, I assume, to the death of Sir Lionel Biscuit?"

"Well, rather. I mean, I could be referring to a general sort of philosophical impression you may have of the world or our existence, but the death of Sir Lionel Biscuit seems decidedly more germane, wouldn't you say?"

"Yes, sir, I perceived it as unlikely you were speaking with an epistemological bent."

"That's rather obtuse of you, Pelham, but I'm just edgy enough to agree with those syllables."

"I am most disturbed at the occurrence, sir. I was in no way fond of Sir Lionel—"

"Well, there's nothing in that, old bean. The man was a rhinoceros."

"Indeed, sir, he was capable of surprising disagreeability. As I say, I was not fond of the gentleman, but the strong possibility of there being a murderer amongst the guests or servants at this house is most distressing."

"Yes, well, 'distressing' is putting it mildly. We could all of us be in danger. Pelham, we must discover the identity of the killer."

"One would expect that to be the duty of the members of the local police force who have assembled below, sir."

"Yes, but you've read detective novels, Pelham. You know how the police are."

"I regret to say I have not read many detective novels, sir. I find myself drawn to more edifying forms of literature."

"Ah, well, that's nothing to be ashamed of, Pelham. We're all men below the surface. But if you'd take the time to peruse one of Mrs. Christie's or Miss Borogove's, then you'd know the police cannot be trusted. They're sure to muck it up."

"Indeed, sir? How would you suggest to proceed?" Pelham had put down the iron and was draping my tuxedo trousers over a lacquered hanger.

"Pelham, we shall best proceed in the manner of Mrs. Christie's Hercule Poirot."

"Poirot, sir?"

"Yes, Poirot's a Belgian detective. Always solving the most deucedly difficult cases, all through the judicious use of his little grey cells."

Pelham turned to look at me. "Little grey cells, sir?"

"Rather."

"This is presumedly a euphemism for the brain, sir?"

"Yes, Pelham, the brain." I tapped my temple in a way that would be best described as "knowingly." "I shall turn the full power of my organ of comprehension to the service of solving this beastly conundrum."

"If I may, sir?"

"Yes, Pelham?"

"Perhaps, sir, in this case Hercule Poirot may not be the most fitting model for you to attempt."

"Ah. I see your point, Pelham. Belgians, what? Perhaps we should proceed along the lines of Sherlock Holmes. He used process of elimination, correct?"

"I am somewhat ambushed by your indiscriminate use of the pronoun 'we.' I believe, however, from what I do know of Sir Arthur Conan Doyle's work, that you are correct as to Mr. Holmes' methods."

"So who could it not be, Pelham? It's not me. It's not, I assume, you."

"No, sir."

"You would tell me if you had murdered someone, wouldn't you Pelham?"

"If I found it necessary for you to be informed, I would not hesitate to do so, sir."

"Ah, good man. So that's two marked off. It probably isn't Skorjenhensen—I just don't think the man has the brains to commit a subtle murder. A full-on throttling with no alibi, yes. But a . . . what was it?"

"I do not think the cause of death has been yet ascertained, sir. Miss Borogove suggested poison, and her reasoning appeared sound. However, there has been no official substantiation of that theory."

"Well, whatever it was, it's not Skorjenhensen's style. I can't imagine it would have been Moony or Arabella."

"Mr. Huffsworthy seemed quite upset with Sir Lionel when he left you this morning, sir. The sight of Miss Biscuit's injuries seemed to galvanize him into action."

"Yes, that's true. It just doesn't seem like Moony, if you see what I mean. He's more the leave-a-terse-but-unsigned-note sort of chap. And Arabella is such a mouse."

"But she is a mouse who has been, it would seem, systematically mistreated. It is not without precedent that meek persons can be pushed, as it were, too far."

I mulled that one. "Okay, Pelham, I must admit to the possibility, however unlikely. We shall table consideration of Arabella for the nonce. Perhaps Signor MacGregor?"

"No, sir."

"No, I suppose not. Who does that leave, then?"

"The servants are left, as well as Lord Huffsworthy."

"Ah, yes, his doleful Lordship. And Mimsy tells me there was a debt being collected this weekend. Lord Huffsworthy bears looking into, Pelham."

"Yes, sir. May I ask, sir. . . ?"

"Yes, Pelham?"

"Do you think it possible that Miss Borogove—"

"I do not, Pelham."

"Just as you say sir. Then perhaps I may make a further suggestion."

"Suggest away, Pelham. You are the Watson to my Holmes, after all."

"You are most kind, sir. I would venture to remind you of the events of last night, and that there is most likely a werewolf among us."

"Ah, yes, Pelham, I had hoped you had quite recovered. You think, I presume, that the werewolf committed the murder?"

"I do not go so far as that, sir. But it is nearly always the case that murders occur because of, or in the service of, secrets."

"Secrets, Pelham?"

"Secrets, sir. And I would further suggest that being a were-wolf is one of the most impressive secrets one could hope to harbor. As you will more than likely discover this evening."

"This evening."

"Yes, sir, at moonrise."

"When I become a wolf."

"Indeed, sir."

"Perhaps, Pelham, we should find Moony."

"As you wish, sir."

Chapter Six

Moony was not in the drawing room, the morning room, the lounge, or the library. Nor was he in the dining room, though there was no reason he should be there. I continued on into the kitchen, a room I did not usually enter, but it was a most unusual day. Who knew where Moony may be?

Moony was not in the kitchen. Dobbins was there, as were the various undercooks and servers assisting him with the delectable lunch he was in the midst of conjuring. I did not want to interrupt the master at work; at any point a Dobbins meal is to be celebrated as if holy, but given the stress of the day, we all needed the exquisite culinary paradise to which only Dobbins could send us. Pure charity work, what the man was doing. I merely said, "Sorry to bother you, Dobbins, I was simply looking for Mr. Huffsworthy. Haven't seen the old bean by any chance, have you?"

Dobbins looked up from a pot bubbling with some Olympian ambrosia that smelled like the culmination of a life well-lived. "I'm sorry, Mr. Spiffington, but I haven't seen Mr. Huffsworthy since we were all in the library. Have you tried his room?"

I had not tried his room. All things considered, Dobbins' suggestion was a good one. I turned to make my exit, but my movement was arrested by Dobbins continuing to speak.

"It is a horrible tragedy, isn't it, Mr. Spiffington?"

"You mean Sir Lionel's death?"

"Of course, sir. I cannot recall anything like it happening in this house in all the years I have served his Lordship. A horrible tragedy."

"Yes, an altogether bad show. I suppose 'tragedy' is a word that would get attached to such an occurrence, regardless of circumstances. 'Horrible' gets bandied about with abandon, I often find, but one does feel sympathy for Miss Biscuit."

"I think I understand you, Mr. Spiffington. If I may be so bold, there are a few of the servants who are not, as you might say, purchasing mourning clothes in response to Sir Lionel's death."

"Yes, well. He was not a fount of sunshine. Still, one wouldn't wish an untimely demise on the man, just because he was mind-numbingly unpleasant."

"Someone did, sir. More than wished it." Dobbins sprinkled a handful of herbs into the steaming righteousness in his pot, whisking and stirring like a god. He glanced up at me as he did so, nearly knowingly.

"Now look here, Dobbins. You aren't suggesting that I—"

"Oh no, sir." He looked shocked, thankfully. "Not at all. I'm only pointing out what the Detective Inspector has already said. *Some*one more than wished Sir Lionel an untimely demise. Someone helped him to it."

"Well, that's just the question, isn't it? Who helped him to it? Are you suggesting some sort of insight into the answer to that question, Dobbins, old boy?"

Once again, Dobbins looked shocked. I realized I'd need to be careful or I'd put him off his cooking. "No, sir! I spend all my time in here, either preparing or clearing up. Unless the murder happened in the kitchen, I'd be very unlikely to know anything about it."

"You haven't overheard any mumblings or rumblings amongst the downstairs set? No parlour-maids or underbutlers making meaningful innuendos concerning the old blighter's mortal coil-shuffling?"

"No, sir. Nothing comes to mind."

"None of the guests or family had expressed any overwhelming desire to murder anyone?"

"Well, no, sir. You don't usually confide in the cook when you're about to commit a murder, do you?"

I was flummoxed by the man's logic. In retaliation I gave him the Spiffington look. Only the aged GF can really do the Spiffington look to perfection, at which point it can actually skim the crust off old cheese, but I can do a fair approximation. I daresay Dobbins was chastened. "I don't murder people, Dobbins," I said severely, "so I can scarcely say how one would behave beforehand."

"Yes, sir. Of course, sir," said Dobbins, suitably demure. "I apologize, sir."

"Not at all, Dobbins, not at all. Now carry on." And I left him there, stirring and herbing and I don't know whating.

I was warming to my new role as amateur detective. I felt my impromptu questioning of Dobbins rather expertly handled. I was simply bursting to share my newfound calling. Due to circumstances, lunch was served in our rooms, an inconvenience more than assuaged by the angelic nature of the meal itself. After sending my tray down with Jane the maidservant, I ventured back out to detect.

I still couldn't find Moony, and having exhausted the possibilities as I saw them, I sought and found Mimsy Borogove, who was sure to assist in my detecting, and who would look scrumptious while so doing. Mimsy was in the god-awful drawing room, which had been cleared of all corpses by the terribly efficient local constabulary. She was looking wistfully out the window, her coppery curls tied back with a pale green ribbon. If I knew my iambic from my triolet, I would have waxed poetic right then and there. Being in general a creature of prose, I merely cleared my throat in an appreciative way.

"Mimsy," I said, "I have begun using my detective powers in the service of discovering the identity of the murderer."

She turned round, her green eyes flashing amusement. "Oh, have you? And how have you done so far?"

"Smashing! I've just been putting the screws to Dobbins. Fairly roasted the poor man on a spit. I daresay he'll recognize shrewdness next time he sees it."

"Oh, wonderful! You found out his whereabouts at the time of the murder, then?"

"Ah. Well, no. That one slipped my mind in the intoxication of the chase."

"Oh. Did you get more information about the blackmailing? I could tell he knew more than he told when we spoke yesterday."

"Dash it! I completely forgot his knowing about that."

"Reggie, darling, whatever did you ask Dobbins?"

"Oh, you know, I asked him where Moony was. And then he sort of implied I might be the murderer. Or perhaps he didn't. And I denied it in the strongest possible terms. He seemed well and truly chastised when I'd done."

"Anything else?"

"He did have some rather unkind things to say about Sir Lionel."

"Well, who doesn't? Reggie dear, I'm afraid I can't give you very high marks as a detective."

"This detecting business is harder than I at first grasped. There are depths, Mimsy, of which I was unaware."

She patted my cheek, but not in a way calculated to set my heart spinning. "My poor dear," she said, "perhaps we'd better do this together. I agree we should try our best to help the police. My experience is that the police need all the help they can get."

"I haven't even seen the police at work. What is Chief Inspector Pail up to?"

"Well, since the little gathering in the library, he's mainly been questioning me."

"You? You mean he actually does suspect you? That's ludicrous!"

"Thank you, Reggie, darling. But one of my great failings is my inability to keep my mouth shut. I talked about poison out loud, and I very publically accused the victim of stealing my manuscript, as you pointed out."

"But it's preposterous! You are no murderer, Mimsy. I'll have a word or two with the Chief Inspector—why, I was with you beforehand to within ten minutes of the blighter being discovered!"

"Don't worry, Reggie. I'm sure I can take care of myself. But I certainly wouldn't mind discovering the true killer's identity.

Shall we detect?" And here she held out her arm to me as if we were attending a ball. "Who shall we see first?"

And then I had a remembrance. A lurking Sherlock in the old Spiffington brainpan recalled my conversation with Fitchly Skorjenhensen on the tennis court that morning. "We should talk with Mr. Skorjenhensen," I said to my emerald-eyed temptress. "He was about to tell me something about Sir Lionel. And he made a reference to 'seeing something in the woods' which he didn't take the time to make less vague."

"In the woods? Why was he in the woods?"

"Following me, apparently."

"Why were you in the woods?"

"I was waiting for you, my dear, and preparing to be attacked by a large animal."

"Oh, Reggie I am sorry. But your suggestion is a good one. Let's find Mr. Skorjenhensen."

And so we did. Being directed by the underbutler, we discovered Fitchly Skorjenhensen in the stableyard with Signor Reynaldo MacGregor, grooming Abercrombie, the huge stallion which had so incommoded the roadster as we motored down the previous day. It was a revelation to watch the man and the animal together. Fitchly Skorjenhensen was a different creature altogether as he tended to the big horse. One might almost use the words "tender" or "caring" to describe the attentive manner in which the giant stroked and patted the Clydesdale's coat. True affection is a beauty to behold, even if the brutes involved are the size of Alps.

Upon seeing Mimsy and I sauntering innocuously into the stableyard, Fitchly dropped his curry comb (if that equine appellation can be properly applied to the object with which he was molesting the animal) and stepped protectively in front of the horse. Mimsy looked amusedly from me to Abercrombie and Fitchly and then back again.

"Mr. Skorjenhensen," said Mimsy, "I hardly think Mr. Spiffington is going to harm your horse."

"My Abercrombie is upset by the man's presence," said the huge man. "Just his walking into the yard has put the poor thing all a-tremble." The horse placidly chewed a stalk of grass, otherwise seeming carved of stone except for the occasional tail twitch. I had a brief vision of its life under the overprotective hands of Fitchly Skorjenhensen and felt a momentary twinge of sympathy. It passed, mind you.

"Never fear, old bean," I said. "I'm not here to antagonize your fine steed." I was attempting to put the subject at ease, you understand. "We merely want to talk with you."

"What have we got to talk about? I don't have anything to say to anybody in this horror of a house." Fitchly was red-eyed and still seemed morose. Mimsy noticed as well.

"Mr. Skorjenhensen, I know it must be a horrible blow to lose someone as close as Sir Lionel." She stepped towards him and stroked Abercrombie's nose. "We're all upset by something like this happening among us."

The woman was a wonder. The sympathy in her voice was just the thing. The big man broke down in sobs, sitting down on a rough wooden bench against the stable wall and dropping his massive head into his hands. Mimsy sat next to him and put her hand on his back. "There, now," she said, "I know. It's hard to lose a friend."

Fitchly Skorjenhensen raised his sniffling head, indignant. The scars and bruises on his face stood out in bas-relief, as it were, against the tan of his skin. He looked like a Grecian urn, if I may refer to a well-known poet. "That fat little blighter was no friend of mine!" He spat this out with a low growling vehemence that took me, I must admit, aback. I couldn't help myself, I simply had to ask:

"What the devil are you crying for, then? I thought you were the only mourner on this funereal occasion."

He glowered at me. Really, the man's head was the size of the Albert Memorial. "You!" he said. "You just shut it!" Which wasn't quite an answer, if you see what I mean.

"Reggie didn't put it very delicately," Mimsy said with a thin-eyed glance at me, "but it's a fair question, Mr. Skorjenhensen. If you're not upset at Sir Lionel's death, why *are* you crying?"

"Because my whole life just got shaken up and tossed aside, that's what! All the years I gave to that man, all the 'come here' and 'do that' and 'just beat that person bloody' I put up with.

And for what? I was supposed to marry that darling little girl of his. I was supposed to join the dynasty, he said."

"He used the word 'dynasty'?" I said, and then stepped back in case the look he gave me presaged violence.

"What happened?" asked Mimsy, which was probably the better question, I'll own. "Yesterday it seemed as if he still had you in mind for Arabella. Come to think of it, this morning at breakfast it looked the same."

Skorjenhensen looked scorn upon her. "Oh, is that how it looked, Miss High and Mighty novelist? Well, what you don't know is . . . is . . . well, it's a bloody lot, ain't it?"

"You're saying that Sir Lionel did not intend to marry you to his daughter?" I asked.

"I'm saying that I told him right off last night I wasn't marrying no daughter of his. I wasn't getting mixed up in no dynasty what deals in the sort of things that Sir Lionel does."

"I applaud you, Fitchly old bean," I said. "That shows a strong character. But, if I may ask, what put you off? You seemed thick as what-do-you-call-ems yesterday evening. Lots of companionable chuckling in the smoking room and what-not."

He sat up straighter and looked at me. "Nothing," he said. "I just changed my mind, is all."

"Fitchly," I said, sitting on the other side of him from Mimsy. "This morning on the tennis court you started to tell me something before we were interrupted by the discovery of the body. What did you see in the woods last night?"

He shook his head. "I knew Sir Lionel was a bad'un. There's nothing in that. I've known lots of bad men. But I'd have never guessed . . . Arabella. . . ." He choked back another unmanly sob.

Ah-ha! The underbrush pushed aside for me now. "You saw what he did to Arabella? Don't look at me like that, my man. I know all about Sir Lionel and his daughter."

"I'm not going to talk about it," said Fitchly Skorjenhensen, wide-eyed with horror. "It's too unnatural. As a matter a fact," and here he stood, all twelve miles of him, "I'm not talking to you two at all." He picked up the pick or whisk or whatever it was and tossed it through the open door of the stable. Then he swung his bulk up onto Abercrombie's back. I fancy I heard the poor beast's bones creaking. "I'm going for a ride."

Mimsy stood up. "Mr. Skorjenhensen, wait!" The big man turned his horse and waited. "Can you at least tell us why Sir Lionel came down this weekend? I know it was to claim a debt from Lord Huffsworthy. Do you know what it was?"

Fitchly Skorjenhensen laughed a short bark. "Oh, yeah. I know all about that. He was here to take Dobbins."

My heart seized. "I'm sorry, what did you say?"

"Lord Huffsworthy put his chef up as collateral on a loan to Sir Lionel. The loan was due, and Huffsworthy couldn't pay. So Sir Lionel came down this weekend to claim Dobbins. Don't matter now. Lord Huffsworthy got a miss on that one, ain't he?" He turned Abercrombie and moved towards the fields.

"Wait, Fitchly! Did Dobbins know this?"

"Oh, aye! We told him to start packing the minute we got here. Now let me be, you madman!" And off he galloped.

Mimsy and I looked at each other. "Good lord, Mimsy. That puts an interesting spin on things."

Mimsy opened her mouth to reply, but at that point Signor MacGregor, whom we had forgotten, interrupted her. "The wolf, itsa walk in the woods," he said.

"You seem rather preoccupied with wolves this weekend, Signor," I said, giving him a severe look. I began to suspect him of being in collusion with Pelham. "What do you mean?"

"I justa say. In the woods, the wolf itsa walk."

"Yes, well. I can't thank you enough for your insight. Come, Mimsy." And I steered that peerless jewel out of the stable yard and back towards the house.

Chapter Seven

My list of suspects had suddenly gotten quite a bit shorter. Mimsy and I were divided on the question of Dobbins' involvement (I couldn't imagine an artist on the order of Dobbins lowering himself to such an act), but we both agreed Lord Huffsworthy was simply swimming in motive. Mimsy said she couldn't see any other viable candidates. I said, and here I used a phrase pinched from Mimsy Borogove's own novels, that Lord Huffsworthy was our prime suspect. We knew we needed to find him and put him on the same intellectual rack on which we'd just stretched Fitchly Skorjenhensen. But then, as we walked back towards the house, I had a thought. I know, dear reader, I know. And yet.

"Mimsy," quoth I, "I have a thought."

"Yes, Reggie?" she said in that responsive way of hers.

"This morning, when you pulled me aside to search for your manuscript—"

"Which is still missing—"

"Which is still missing. . . . I was in search of Moony. He himself was in search of Sir Lionel. Moony had just discovered Arabella's unfortunate situation *vis-a-vis* the bruises and what-not, and had gone off in higher dudgeon than I've ever seen him."

"Did he say what his intentions were?"

"He said Sir Lionel was evil, and then he said, 'there's nothing for it then.'"

"Reggie, that doesn't sound good. Do you think that Moony could have killed the man?"

"I shouldn't have thought so, but Pelham feels that when pushed to extremity, even the meekest mouse may rise up against its oppressor."

At this point we were passing the formal gardens, and I could see Moony, seated with Arabella amongst the ornamentals. "Perhaps I'd better sound him out. I haven't properly talked with him since the murder."

"Shall I come with you, Reggie?" She said this in an irritating "will-you-ask-the-right-questions" sort of way.

"No, my dear, I think I have this one well in hand. I've known Moony since we were but lads. I can handle him with ease."

"All right then," she said reluctantly. "I'll go and see if I can find Lord Huffsworthy."

I entered the formal gardens with an innocent flourish, hands behind my back and a welcoming smile on the old lips. I could smell the various flowering bushes and fruity vines that constituted the gardens of Huffsworthy Hall, and which seemed to be frightfully odorous this morning. Moony and Arabella were seated on an ornate bench beneath a rose arbor. They were holding hands, the sly little lovebirds, but jumped guiltily apart upon my approach. Moony stood and greeted me.

"Ah, Reggie! Arabella and I were just talking about you."

"Really? And what, pray, were you saying, Moony old boy?"

"That it was good to be surrounded by friends in the midst of a difficult time."

"Oh, well, I'm glad I could help. I was wondering how the two of you were doing. Miss Biscuit, I'm terribly sorry for your loss. It's a rum thing, murder."

Arabella Biscuit looked a little less noodly this afternoon, but perhaps it was just the effect of the westering sun on her otherwise colorless hair. "Thank you, Mr. Spiffington." She looked decidedly uncomfortable.

"Arabella feels guilty," said Moony. "She knows she ought

to be upset by her father's murder, but, well. You know what her father was."

"It is hard to deny a sense of relief, Mr. Spiffington," added Arabella. "I'm afraid I'm not a very good person."

Moony sat by her again and squeezed her hand. "Nonsense, my darling," he said. "You are the best of girls."

"How are you taking it, Moony old bean?" I asked. "Murder in your father's house. Bit of a scandal, what?"

"Oh, that'll be all right, I suppose. Daddy can stand it. He must be relieved as well."

"Yes, I suppose so. I say, Moony, old man, where did you run off to when you left us in the library this morning?"

"I . . . what? You mean before the murder?"

"Well, I mean before the discovery of the body at any rate. You were fairly upset at Arabella's bruises. I beg your pardon, Miss Biscuit." Arabella shook her head that it was all right. "I'd go so far as to call you 'fierce' if it wasn't a sort of unMoony word. Did you see Sir Lionel before the, um?"

"Reggie, do you suspect me of murdering the father of my one true love?" Moony looked truculent, if that isn't a word for a type of hollandaise.

"Moony, I have known you from time immemorial. I have never thought you capable of causing a moment's discomfort to even the smallest and most irritating of God's creatures. I do not suspect you of murdering Sir Lionel Biscuit."

"Well, I should hope not. Thank you, Reggie."

"But I must say that your going off in search of the man with your eyes flashing fire, or at least static electricity, just before he is found dead won't look very cricket to Chief Inspector Pail."

"But the police know where I went after I left you."

"Where?"

"I called the police!"

"You called . . . you mean you're the one who called the police? *That's* why they arrived so quickly after the body had been found?"

"Well, yes. They were coming in response to my call. I wanted something done about Sir Lionel."

"I see. And what did you do after calling the police?"

"I, uh, well, you see I . . ." and here Moony turned positively pink. He was saved by Arabella Biscuit, who firmly interrupted him.

"He was with me, in my room."

"In your room?" I asked. To say my jaw hit the ground would be anatomical hyperbole, but I was both aghast and agog. I'm no prude, if you see what I mean, but I didn't think either of them had the foresight or wherewithal.

"Archibald came to make sure I was all right and to tell me he had called the authorities," Arabella said. "And then he stayed." Moony looked as nearly balanced between pride and chagrin as it is possible to be. Arabella took his hand. "And I'm perfectly willing to tell the police as much if they suspect my sweet Archibald." Well, well. Points for the Noodle.

"Well, that's both of you taken care of, then." I said. "Mimsy suspects Dobbins, and I'm worried that your father may . . . " But here I left my verb a-dangle, for my nose had caught a whiff of something that stopped me in my tracks. It was the odd gardeny smell I had caught wind of in the room with Sir Lionel's body. It wasn't exactly a flowery odor, but it was certainly plantish and it was certainly somewhere nearby. I looked around, sniffing for the source.

"Worried that my father may what?" asked Moony. I didn't answer right away, as I was worried I'd lose the scent if I paused or quit concentrating. We were in a little walled nook within the larger garden, and I began to move around the place, sniffing as I went. Moony and Arabella followed me with creased brows.

"I say, Reggie, have you got a cold?" asked Moony. "You aren't about to sneeze on the lupines, are you?"

And then I found it. A tall plant with rows of flowers like little purple bells. It was a deucedly good-looking flower, but I couldn't remember seeing any in the drawing room with Sir Lionel's body. "That's what I'm smelling," I said.

Moony sniffed. "I can't smell anything," he said. "Are you feeling all right, Reggie?"

"I'm feeling right as rain, Moony, old chum," I said. "What are these flowers?"

"I don't know. I've never been one for botanical names and what-not. We have a gardener for that. They're very pretty."

"Yes. I only wondered."

"It's foxglove," said Arabella. "Purple foxglove." She was looking at me strangely with her watery eyes. "Can you really smell them?"

"I must be smelling something else," I said. This was a lie, you see, because I was beginning to be concerned about this nose business. "But I do like these. I think I'll cut a couple for Miss Borogove. If you don't mind, Moony?"

"I don't mind," said Moony.

I bent down and snapped two plants off towards the base of the stems. As I did so, a brace of flowers behind the foxglove, bluish flowers a little lower down, caught my nose and my eye. And I'm jiggered if I know how to explain it, but I felt a strong sense of repulsion. Not quite as strong as if my aged grandfather Hammerthorpe Q. Spiffington had turned up and tried to give me a familial hug, but a damn sight close. I even recoiled, yes an actual recoiling, if you can credit that. Moony and Arabella were still watching me strangely, so I attempted to explain my jumpiness by shouting "Snake!" and then pretending I had mistaken a climbing ivy for an adder.

"Sorry," I said. "I'm a little jumpy after last night."

"Why?" asked Arabella. "What happened last night?"

"Oh, I forgot, in all the uproar this morning I neglected to mention. I was attacked by a big dog last night in the clearing south of the house."

"A dog? Were you hurt?" She looked terribly concerned.

"Scratched up my arm a bit. Much better today, thanks."

Moony, bless him, was also concerned for me. "Reggie, how awful! I'll tell Daddy. He can have our man Randall go out with a gun and—"

"No!" I said, surprisingly forcefully. "I mean to say, it's just a scratch really. I shouldn't have been mucking about the woods in the middle of the night. It stands to reason that a fellow will end up . . . " And here, as evidenced by my use of the ellipsis, most vague and unfinished of punctuations, I trailed off. For I suddenly had a vision of Fitchly Skorjenhensen's scarred and bruised face, coupled with a memory of Pelham whacking away at a huge wolf with his umbrella. And even though I knew I was being led by Pelham's pipe through the Hamelin streets of insanity, I asked anyway.

"Arabella," I said. "Fitchly Skorjenhensen says he saw you and your father in the woods last night. He wouldn't talk about it really."

"Why would I have been in the woods last night?" asked the Noodle. "I don't know what Fitchly was doing last night, or what he thinks he saw."

I realized too late that if Fitchly had seen Arabella being mistreated by her father, as he had seemed to indicate, then of course she would be reticent to discuss it. It goes to show how rattled the whole day had gotten me, as I'm normally much more astute. "Yes, well. I only report what the great wall of Sweden said to me. I can in no way vouch for his veracity, as it were."

I left the two lovers there in the garden, promising to see them at the dinner table in ninety minutes or so. As tiring and unlikely as it seems, my mind continued to work as I walked towards the house and made my way back to my room. I was distressed by something, friends and supporters, and that something was Pelham's maddening fairy tales. The vague idea swirling around in the old bean seemed to connect the dots between Fitchly Skorjenhensen and Pelham's ideas about werewolves loose on the Huffsworthy grounds. It would explain Fitchly's battered visage, his presence in the woods last night, and the bloody great bite to the arm I had gotten in lieu of a picnic. But this line of thinking also raised some uncomfortable questions, such as why Arabella seemed evasive about seeing Fitchly the previous evening. Did she know about this lupine aspect? And did my being bitten actually mean, as Pelham suggested *ad nauseum*, that I . . . But that way lies madness, you see.

I entered the house and shut the door upon thoughts of werewolves. That was a metaphor, though I did, you understand, shut the door. I moved through the hall towards the stairs, and as I did so, Bugsby the Butler (whose neatly alliterative appellation makes one want to mention his name endlessly; or perhaps that was just me) emerged from the library and saw me.

"Mr. Spiffington," he said, correctly identifying me in the efficient manner of all good butlers, "perhaps you would like a vase for your bouquet?" He raised his eyebrows at the foxglove in my hand. Bugsby was not a talkative individual; in fact the preceding speech was possibly the most I'd ever heard him speak at once.

"Thank you, Bugsby, but no. They're a gift, and I'd rather hand them over as is. Easier to flourish them and all that."

"I see, sir. Sorry to have troubled you." He turned to go.

"Oh, Bugsby?"

"Yes, Mr. Spiffington?" He had half-turned back to me, poised like an ice-skater in the marble hallway.

"I say, it's a rum thing, this murder."

He considered this. "Yes, Mr. Spiffington."

"How are you taking it?"

"How am I taking it, sir?"

"Yes, you know, a murder happening in the house where you are butler in charge. Bit disconcerting, what?"

"I assure you I know nothing about Sir Lionel's death, Mr. Spiffington."

"I never said you did, old man. I merely suggested that—"

"I am fully aware that in many detective novels, like those written by Miss Borogove, the servants are often implicated. I can vouch for my whereabouts all morning."

"I have no doubts on the matter at all."

"I cannot express how tiresome it is to always hear that 'the butler did it.' When a half-way decent butler would have time to commit a murder is beyond me."

"It is an affront to common sense. I'll speak to Miss Borogove as a representative of detective novelists the world over."

"Thank you, sir."

"Not at all. I don't suppose you have any idea who might have wanted Sir Lionel out of the way? Since we're on the subject?"

"I am sure I cannot help you, Mr. Spiffington. Everyone and no one is my answer."

"I'm not sure I follow you, old chap. Those phrases are antonyms, you see."

"I mean to imply, Mr. Spiffington, that nearly everyone who

met Sir Lionel Biscuit disliked him to the point of violence. But I cannot imagine anyone in this house actually committing a murder. This is Huffsworthy Hall."

"Of course. I understand that Huffsworthy Hall is a respectable house. I intended no disrespect to your domain here."

"Thank you, Mr. Spiffington."

"But you will admit a murder has happened?"

"Regrettably, it is undeniable." He produced a white cloth and began vigorously rubbing a carved wooden horse that stood on a small table by the library door.

"Then it stands to reason in at least one case, you have misjudged the inhabitants of the house. Have you heard nothing that might provide a light in this darkness?" I found this a delicate and beautiful metaphor, but butler Bugsby seemed not to.

"I have heard many people say things against Sir Lionel. You yourself described him and Mr. Skorjenhensen as 'hideous people' while at the breakfast table this morning."

"Yes, well, I would expect support from all his acquaintances in that description."

"Just so, Mr. Spiffington, you have made my point."

I left him still polishing the poor wooden horse, not sure if I had actually had a conversation. Mounting the staircase, I travelled roomward.

Mimsy was in my room. This would normally have made me much happier than the present moment, as Pelham was also there. The two had been comparing notes, as it were. Mimsy had told Pelham the gist of our conversation with Fitchly Skorjenhensen. Pelham had been canvassing the below-stairs set, talking in quick succession with the housekeeper (an unimaginative lorry of a woman called Matilda Nooseheim), the underbutler (called Francis), and Sir Lionel's personal valet Mr. Smythe. The Huffsworthy servants were unhelpful, not through unwillingness to assist but due to lack of anything like information. Mr. Smythe was a more interesting character. Though he didn't seem to have any information pertinent to the murder, Mr. Smythe was found to be completely aware of the animosities of the other guests towards his employer, and of the various motives of each of them for having such feelings.

"I wouldn't have thought, Pelham," I remarked, "that a competent professional such as Mr. Smythe would remain in the employ of someone whom he knows to have such an effect on others."

"Mr. Smythe is neither competent nor a professional, sir."

"I say, Pelham, that's rather straightforward of you."

"In matters of my profession, sir, I feel no compunction in calling a spade a spade. Mr. Smythe would appear to have not had the advantage of proper training, and being in the sort of household in which he has been serving has apparently encouraged attitudes and behaviors unbecoming in a gentleman's gentleman."

"Such as what, Pelham? I must admit to my interest being piqued."

"I'd rather not say, sir. Perhaps it would suffice if I mentioned there were shoes in the room apparently belonging to Sir Lionel that were in a state less than desirable. I found it difficult to focus on Mr. Smythe's statements while in the presence of muddy footwear."

"Must have been terrible for you, old man."

"I seem to have survived, sir, though I thank you for your possibly facetious concern."

"Pelham," said Mimsy, pushing a stray curl behind her ear, "is it possible Mr. Smythe killed Sir Lionel? It must have been hard being personal valet to such a beast."

"I do not believe so, Miss Borogove. Mr. Smythe is certainly an affront to all that is noblest in my profession, but he did not seem to regard his situation as unpleasant. Indeed, he expressed strong regret at Sir Lionel's death and consternation at losing what he perceived as a 'plum job.' The man is nearly cockney in his enthusiasm."

"Oh, bother," I said, "then your time was for all intents wasted."

"Not entirely, sir. Mr. Smythe did inform me that Sir Lionel had travelled here this weekend with the intention of claiming Lord Huffsworthy's chef Dobbins for his own household, Dobbins having been placed as collateral to a loan Lord Huffsworthy had taken from Sir Lionel some time ago."

"Well, not to throw cold what-do-you-call-it on the only fish in your dragnet, Pelham, but Mimsy and I have already heard that from the Swedish horseman."

"Yes, but Pelham has independently verified that information," said Mimsy. "Which is fairly important since we got it from someone who is hardly reliable."

"Well, there is that. I mean, I was taking that as a given. Bugsby was unhelpful in the extreme."

"Was he unhelpful on purpose?" asked Mimsy.

"Oh, I don't think so. He just didn't have anything to tell us, and he was so concerned about the Hall being the site of a murder that he began polishing things. And that leaves us back where we were, yes? Lord Huffsworthy seems a prime suspect. Were you able to find his Lordship, Mimsy?"

"No, unfortunately. He was sequestered with Detective Inspector Mutton. We shall have to attempt him later."

Pelham here interjected, if I may venture a hypodermic grammatical construction. "If I may, sir? It would seem Dobbins himself is as much under suspicion as Lord Huffsworthy. If Sir Lionel was indeed poisoned, and I concur with Miss Borogove's conclusion that he was, then his death roughly forty-five minutes after breakfast this morning should make us question who had access to the breakfast as it was prepared. Dobbins had definite motive, as I would imagine avoiding employ as Sir Lionel's chef would be a particularly strong incentive."

"Do you really think so? It does so upset my sense of the world to suspect Dobbins of murder. Mimsy, you are an expert on crime. Don't you feel Dobbins is too obvious? Couldn't this be a thingy? American phrase. A 'frame-up job,' what?" Even as I asked her, though, my mind was retracing Dobbin's earlier words about Sir Lionel. The man had definitely disliked the baronet.

But Mimsy was not attending to me. She had noticed the flowers I had brought in with me from the garden, which I had rather impetuously tossed on to the bed as I had entered. They lay there, purple and glorious if a little wilty, half-covered by my coat.

"What is that?" she asked.

"Oh. I brought them for you." I retrieved them, realizing

how unromantic the situation was. "When I beheld their pristine beauty in the afternoon light slanting through the leaves, my thoughts all turned to you." I held the two stalks laden with purple flowers out towards Mimsy. She did not take them.

"Reggie, you've brought me foxglove," she said, continuing to not take them from me. I began to feel a bit of a fool.

"I'm sorry about the odd smell of them," I said. "But it's a beauty of a plant, isn't it?"

"There's no smell to speak of. But it's a remarkable plant, certainly." She squinted thoughtfully at the flowers, remaining otherwise unmoving.

"Are we perhaps not at the flower-bringing stage?" I asked.

She finally looked up at my face, concentration broken. "Oh, Reggie, I'm sorry. They're lovely." She reached out and took the foxglove from me. "I was just thinking about its other qualities."

"As was I, Miss Borogove," said my valet. "Do you think perhaps?"

"I suppose it's possible, Pelham. It would fit the bill, wouldn't it?"

"I believe it would meet all of the requirements of the situation to a nicety," said Pelham.

"I say," I said, "you don't go on like that, you know. I am standing rather centrally located in the midst of your floral *tete-a-tete*."

"This is purple foxglove," said Mimsy, brandishing the bouquet, "which is the source of digitalis. Doctors use it to treat heart problems, but they have to be careful with dosage. It's a deadly poison."

"How deadly?" I asked.

"Well, dead is dead, isn't it?"

"Yes, but. There are 'I'm feeling rather unwell but it may take a couple of days' deadlies and then there are 'I feel as if I may fall over within the next three or four minutes' deadlies."

"This is a sort of 'I'll be dead after forty-five minutes of absurdly painful stomach cramps, possibly with vomiting' deadly."

"You're awfully knowledgeable about the beastly things, Mimsy!"

"I write crime novels, darling. I know my poisons. I killed the Earl of Shrewsbury with foxglove in *Salad Days*. It's worth noting that Lord Huffsworthy has these in his gardens."

"Begod, Mimsy. Crikey. Do you mean to say you think Sir Lionel may have—"

"It can't be discounted, Reggie. This is readily available in the garden, and Sir Lionel had about forty-five minutes between breakfast and discovery."

"Who would have put foxglove in his food?"

"That returns the line of questioning to its beginning," said Pelham. "If Sir Lionel was poisoned, who possessed both motive and opportunity?"

"Crumbs. It does not look good for Dobbins, does it?"

"I am afraid not, sir. Though it is hardly an airtight case."

"And at any rate," said Mimsy, "foxglove could be a coincidence. I thank you for them Reggie. I can't say they elicit romantic feelings in me given the circumstances, but you have given us something else to think about. I think now, though, that I had better dress for dinner." And the extraordinary woman kissed my cheek as she left the room. Pelham pretended not to notice by turning to pull out the tuxedo.

I contemplated Pelham whilst he readied my dinner clothes. As I watched him work, I considered the joy of having a skilled manservant, and that thought led back to Pelham's comments about Mr. Smythe's shortcomings as a butler.

"Pelham, did you say that Sir Lionel's boots were muddy?"

"The footwear in question were shoes, sir, not boots, but yes, they were exceedingly soiled. The leather along the sides was scuffed and marred, and great clumps of dried mud clung to the soles. It was this overt failing on the part of Mr. Smythe that substantiated my opinion that he is less than what could be desired in regard to the profession."

"Mucky, were they?"

"Yes, sir. There is perhaps a direction in which your questions tend?"

"Something that brute Skorjenhensen said. He saw something in the woods last night, apparently something to do with Sir Lionel. It didn't strike me until now—why would Sir Lionel be in the woods at all? Doesn't it seem a rum thing that Sir Lionel would be traipsing around the wilderness after dark?"

"You yourself were 'traipsing' sir, as was Mr. Skorjenhensen."

"Yes, but I had an appointment, and I can hardly imagine Sir Lionel in a tryst with anyone here. And Skorjenhensen was following me, so he had, as it were, the same reason for being out there."

"Perhaps he muddied his shoes at an earlier time, sir."

"No, that doesn't follow, Pelham. Sir Lionel drove in yesterday afternoon, as we all did, and we are aware of his movements in the house during the afternoon and evening, due to his marked volubility and general bullish behavior. And no matter how poor a butler is our man Smythe, I can't see him packing muddy shoes to bring, what?"

"No, sir. Your reasoning appears sound."

"I believe we should make inquiries, Pelham. Sir Lionel has been up to activities which, by their occurring after nightfall and in the forested environs of the outdoors, could very possibly be nefarious."

"I could re-interrogate Mr. Smythe, sir."

"Perhaps. But I don't want suspicions to be raised."

"Suspicions as to what, sir?"

"Pelham, leave this to those of us who have wherewithal and happenstance."

"Indeed, sir. I did not mean to trespass."

"For now, let us simply dress for dinner."

I began to prepare the Spiffington frame with the tie and tails, but I'll admit to a trenchant thoughtfulness. Two people had now told me purple foxglove held no strong smell, and yet I could still nose out traces of the horrid poisonous fronds even after Mimsy had removed them from the room. I had smelled bacon this very morning at a time when no bacon was cooking, according to Lord Huffsworthy, which meant I smelled uncooked bacon across several rooms and up a flight of stairs. As I listened, beyond the sound of my own toilette, I could hear other members of the household in their own rooms, moving up and down stairs, dressing and talking all over the house. Straining, I could hear what I assumed to be Fitchly Skorjenhensen walking along the side of the house, moving from the stables to the side door, returning from his ride. I had to admit that my hearing may have been heightened to this level for most of the day; I so regularly disregard other people's noises unless they direct them at me that I could well have missed it. I freely own that I was disconcerted.

"Pelham," I finally allowed myself to say, "I have some hypotheticals to pose you."

"Yes, sir?"

"Suppose a chap suddenly found himself able to smell and hear things far beyond the norm? Uncooked bacon, foxglove at forty paces, that sort of thing? Just as a test case for discussion?"

"Well, sir, if I were to consider a hypothetical case such as the one you have put to me, I would conclude that you are a werewolf."

"I say! That's offside!"

"I beg your pardon, sir?"

"Offside. It's a metaphor invoking—"

"I am conversant with the rules of football, sir. I failed to understand your objection to my statement."

"You are not being properly hypothetical, Pelham. I am not a werewolf. I merely wondered how to approach a situation, supposing." Pelham set down the spats he had been preparing.

"Sir. I have hesitated until this point to assert myself beyond employer/employee proprietary boundaries. But the situation moves swiftly towards the inevitable. You have been bitten by a werewolf. You are manifesting evidence of heightened aural and olfactory powers. I would in other circumstances allow you to discover for yourself what these things collectively mean, especially as you seem reticent to accept my informed conclusions on the subject. But if you are in this house at moonrise, the situation will become decidedly unhypothetical, and many people, several of whom you care about, will be in great danger."

Well, dear reader, I mean to say. It had been a day of shocking events, but the experience of being lectured by Pelham was, well, actually I've often been lectured by Pelham. But this moved beyond lecture and deucedly near remonstration. I would have summoned a huff in which to leave, but for the fact the man was so clearly in earnest and for my knowledge, gained through time and experience, that whatever it cost me to be remonstrated by Pelham, it cost Pelham much more to speak in such a manner to his employer. And I might add, if I was so inclined, I was becoming somewhat worried about the very issues of which he spoke.

"Great danger?" I said. "I would be a danger to those I cared about?"

"You would, as I feel you must now understand, be a wolf. Wolves are dangerous animals, and I would conjecture that a wolf who finds himself in a large manor-house surrounded by people is on the more dangerous end of a continuum."

"So, a werewolf does not have control over his actions? I mean, while actually a wolf?"

"I am afraid I don't know the answer to that question, sir."

"I thought you knew about these things, Pelham! I thought you had encountered all manner of beasties!"

"Prior to this weekend, I have only actually seen one werewolf. I was unable to ask him for extensive information about his condition."

"I see. Bit awkward, what?"

"No, sir. The main obstacle was the werewolf being shot by a group of villagers whose views on lycanthropy were less than tolerant."

"Oh. Well, dash it. What *can* you tell me?"

"I am aware of several pieces of information that could possibly be useful. Lycanthropes, which is the scientific term for werewolves—"

"That's a tad oxymoronic, what? 'Scientific term for werewolves.'"

"Are you perhaps uninterested in the information I am attempting to convey, sir?"

"Sorry, Pelham. Please continue."

"Lycanthropes, as I say, begin their transformation at moonrise during the three days surrounding the full moon—that is to say, the night of the full moon and the nights immediately before and after. Tonight is the actual full moon. I have taken the liberty of consulting the almanac, and we may expect the moon to rise at approximately nine o'clock this evening."

"It begins at moonrise and lasts until . . . "

"Until sunrise, sir. During this time, the lycanthrope becomes a wolf physically, though as I say I am unaware of how his or her consciousness is affected. Behavior would seem to indicate that animal instincts hold sway."

"Well, the blighter that went for my throat last night certainly seemed less than civil."

"Indeed, sir. And the unfortunate young man I spoke of earlier, who was shot by villagers, also confirms this hypothesis."

"Bit growly in the night, eh?"

"He did have a disturbing habit of killing and eating sheep, sir."

"Well, yuck, Pelham. I mean to say."

"Yes, sir. As you've seen, lycanthropes heal more quickly than humans—"

"Ah, ah, ah! They heal more quickly than *other* humans."

"I am sorry, sir. They heal more quickly than other humans. But this does not mean they cannot be injured, and depending on the severity of the wound they may still manifest evidence of an injury a fair amount of time into the next morning. It is terribly difficult to kill a lycanthrope, however, and special equipment is often needed."

"I say, who said anything about killing anybody?"

"The information is important, sir. Werewolves are not welcomed by polite society, as evidenced by my anecdote about the villagers."

"So, is it just like in the old stories? Silver bullets, what?"

"Just so, sir. Silver appears to be anathema to lycanthropes, as do various herbs."

"Various herbs? I am loath to ask, Pelham, but is one of those herbs a low-growing jobby with bluish flowers?"

"Very possibly, sir. Your vague description could be reasonably applied to the plant known as monkshood or wolfsbane. It is a powerful repellant to werewolves. Why do you ask?"

"Oh, nothing. It seems the gardens themselves are in on this conspiracy. You know, Pelham, if it were not for Sir Lionel's murder, I'd think this whole weekend was a sort of elaborate practical joke."

"I fail to perceive the humor, sir. The situation is exceedingly serious."

"I'm just still having a hard time swallowing all of this, Pelham. I mean, I've been called a 'wolf' more than once, usually by fellows in the grip of a rather justified envy, but you don't expect to actually be . . . I mean to say, there are limits. It hardly seems natural, does it?"

"It is *super*natural, sir. Or perhaps preternatural."

"Prehensile?"

"Preternatural. Some who have knowledge of these things argue that lycanthropy is an extreme of nature, but not magical or divine in substance."

"Not magical? Turning into a bloody great wolf?"

"I merely report opinions, sir."

"What do you recommend, Pelham? I admit this is beyond my knowledge of etiquette."

"I would suggest," and here Pelham had fully ceased being a valet and had become something much more essential, "that you take every precaution possible to ensure you are far away from the house by the time the moon rises."

Chapter Eight

Dinner was a subdued affair. The suspicions Mimsy and Pelham had raised concerning Dobbins significantly interfered with my enjoyment of the fare on offer, as I spent most of the meal attempting to detect the odor of foxglove in the sauce. I freely admit a certain moodiness and a tendency to glower. I divided my time between eyeing Lord Huffsworthy through the new lens of blackmail victim and watching the increasingly odd behavior of Fitchly Skorjenhensen, whose scratched and bruised visage had gained a habit of firing off furtive and surly glances at anyone within eyeshot. Arabella and Moony were cozier than ever, but the Noodle kept giving me searching once-overs. I once again wondered what Fitchly had seen and how much Arabella knew about what I thought I knew. After the standard greetings, no one spoke.

I found I couldn't finish my food, which smelled tasty but all of which was overdone. That, coupled with my increased awareness of poison, put me quite off my feed. I was just pushing away a full plate of fish when Mimsy elbowed me under the table. I did not yelp, as Mimsy rather slanderously suggested later, but I did utter a sort of half-suppressed cry of surprise. Mimsy nodded at Lord Huffsworthy, who was rising to leave.

"You will all excuse me, I hope," said the Doleful. "I must

see to the arrangements for Signor MacGregor." Reynaldo MacGregor had been scheduled to oblige us with an impromptu program, and even in light of the unfortunate events of the morning, this event was moving forward. "We have moved the performance from the drawing room to the conservatory, and I must see that the piano has been properly placed. I trust I will see you all in half an hour."

He turned to leave the room, and Mimsy elbowed me again. I was ready for her this time, and released not a whimper. "Reggie," she whispered, "follow him! Now's your chance to question him." And she all but shoved me out of my chair. The entire weekend seemed designed for indignities. I followed Lord Huffsworthy into the hall.

"I say, your Lordship, do you have the briefest of moments?" I asked, all smiles. Mostly, at any rate.

He turned to regard me, raising his pince-nez to do so in the real old school manner. "Mr. Spiffington. I am in a hurry, you see."

"Yes, your lordship, and I do apologize. Frightful imposition. I merely wanted to ask you a few questions about Sir Lionel."

"About? Why would you have questions for me about Sir Lionel? Sir Lionel is dead."

"Yes, your lordship, and since his death I have encountered rumors about his intentions in coming here this weekend. It was those I wished to talk with you about. Won't take a moment."

"I am afraid I haven't the time right now, Mr. Spiffington. I can't see how it would be relevant." He turned again to go.

"Your lordship! I just want to confirm whether or not Sir Lionel was attempting to blackmail you . . . " Again with the ellipsis, you see. For the man's face quite precipitated a trailing off of the Spiffington filibuster.

"You are correct, Mr. Spiffington," he said.

"I am?"

"Quite. It *is* a frightful imposition." And he turned on his heel, a balletic feat perfected by lords of the manor both hither and yon, and left the hall.

Dinner had broken up by the time I returned to the dining room, though not everyone had left the premises. In fact, as I approached the door, I saw something which gave me a decided pause, such that I lingered near the half-open door to get a better idea of what I was seeing. Arabella and Fitchly were standing by the French doors, close together and apparently in the midst of a quiet and earnest conversation. Skorjenhensen's considerable bulk blocked most of Arabella's body from view—really the man was like Hadrian's Wall—but it appeared that her hand was on his arm and her face turned up to his. What the devil?

I coughed. Fitchly Skorjenhensen turned, and Arabella fairly leapt away from him, blushing as hard as she could, which was quite hard, truth be told.

"The concert is about to begin," I said.

"Of course," said Arabella. "I don't want to be late!" and she flitted from the room at speed. I remained behind, looking questioningly at the Swede.

"What the bloody hell do you think you're looking at?" he asked, ever the charmer.

"Just curious what sort of *tête à tête* you were having with the woman you described as 'no wife of yours' earlier today."

"Oh, that," he said, chuckling in that sinister manner I found so endearing, "that's no mystery. That's none of your ruddy business!" And then he stomped from the room as well, leaving me none the wiser.

Mimsy sat next me at the concert, but we were both distracted by the sense of iniquity that permeated the approaching evening like water in a sponge, if you will excuse a damp metaphorical flourish. The performance began. Arabella Biscuit had been slated to accompany the Signor on the piano, but given that her father was less than twelve hours dead, a concession was made. Thus, Signor MacGregor found himself singing against the valiant plinkings of Archibald Huffsworthy III, who assaulted the pianoforte in a manner not unlike a slug climbing a salt shaker. There was a sense of tentativeness in the face of which the whole project began to dry up. Moony touched the keys as if they might bite, and the instrument responded by making soft little noises of pain.

I was concerned by the scene I had witnessed in the dining room, and further concerned by the fixedness with which

Arabella Biscuit avoided acknowledging or even glancing in the direction of Fitchly Skorjenhensen. Could her mooning over Moony have been mere pretense? Was there actually some sort of understanding between her and the large unpleasant Swede, both of their avowals notwithstanding? The mind boggled, dear reader, and frankly the stomach churned.

My mood was not improved by Signor MacGregor's choice of program. The first piece was a *lied* by Hugo Wolf, which seemed a coincidence I could have done without. But then he chose to perform two pieces from the Red Riding Hood opera currently all the rage in London. Both of these pieces are sung by the Big Bad Wolf, who pleads for understanding in the first and talks about how tasty Red looks in the second. As Reynaldo MacGregor's howling faded away, I mopped the brow a bit, I'll admit. Luckily the next piece was more standard fare— Pulchinelli's "Variations on 'I'm a Little Teapot,'"—and I was able to relax somewhat. And with my relative relaxation, I became aware of other aspects of the room, some not nearly as off-putting as Signor MacGregor's wolf songs.

I was very aware, for instance, of Mimsy sitting beside me. She was warm and soft and very much there, if you see what I mean. My sense of smell had continued its mad prowess-increasing progress, and Mimsy smelled quite lovely. My animal instincts were definitely aroused, as it were, and I found myself wishing the concert would end so I could take Mimsy somewhere and bat things around.

No sooner thought than done. Signor MacGregor was bowing to the polite applause of the few of us in the room, Fitchly Skorjenhensen betraying none of the ox-like confusion he had evidenced whilst listening to the show. Then we were wandering out into the hall, and I was pulling Mimsy by the arm into the library.

"Reggie, darling, whatever are you up to?"

But I was having none of that. I pulled her into my arms and pressed my lips fervently, and I do not use the word lightly, to hers. She tasted of cigarettes and wine, and seemed not at all displeased at my impetuosity. Indeed, after lifting my head for a quick breath, I dove in afresh, and was rewarded by Mimsy's arms reciprocating around my neck. She was just the height, really. Much shorter and I'd have risked pulling my sciatica, and whether we admit or not, tall women oughtn't. Mimsy should and, if I may say so, does. With aplomb.

I had scarcely gotten started when Mimsy pushed me back to arm's length. "Reggie, oh Reggie! We can't—not here. Anyone could walk in on us here in the library."

"Where do you suggest?" I growled.

"I think we should try for picnic redux."

I growled again.

"The sun has gone down now. Give me ten minutes and I'll meet you at the clearing in the woods again. I think if we try the side door past the conservatory we may be able to avoid the police. Oh, Reggie!" She kissed me again, in the hollow beneath my jaw. And then I thought two things. One: why had I never noticed how perfectly delightful the hollow beneath my jaw was? Two: had I actually growled just now?

I took in the scene we presented. I had pressed Mimsy up against the wall behind the library door. My jacket was half off, and I had somehow pulled her scarf to the floor and had placed my hands . . . crumbs! Hands do fit some places better than others. Egad! This wasn't like me at all. Right here in the library where anyone could walk in on us? Despite her protests, Mimsy didn't really seem to mind (a fact which I have even now filed away for future use), but that wasn't the point. What was the point?

"No," I said, imbuing that single syllable with every ounce of self-control I could muster. "That's, that's not a good idea this evening, Mimsy, darling."

She looked so saddened, so diminished by my refusal that I nearly recanted. But, I had need to be strong. "I'm sorry, dear," I continued. "I can't get away tonight. And I'm worried the murderer may still be among us."

"Oh," she said. "But I shouldn't worry if we were together. I thought you—"

"I do. I think it's safe to say I do more than I can decorously express. But these are unique circumstances and I feel we need to err on the side of caution."

"Shall I come to your room?"

"N–no. I believe it best that we—please stop doing that, Mimsy—that we be vigilant this evening."

She stopped what she was doing. "You're serious, aren't you?"

"I am afraid so, my darling. It's not never, it's just tonight."

"Why, Reggie, I've never known you to be so thoughtful and serious. And I must say it doesn't make the situation any easier for me. It's very attractive, this seriousness." She gazed up at me. I didn't know what to say. "Well, darling, if you must be the adult then I support you. But this picnic is going to be quite worth waiting for when it does happen. Trust me." I believe she actually smoldered at me. This was like climbing Mount Everest.

"I want to ask a favor of you, Mimsy."

"Of course, Reggie. Whatever you'd like."

"I want you to promise me you will stay inside this evening. That you won't go outside, not even into the garden for a breath of air."

She laughed, but then saw something in my face that must have shown I was in earnest. Also, I'm quite handsome. "Why, Reggie, you strange man. All right, if you insist on being so protective, I promise." She kissed me again.

"I think I may retire to my room," I said. "It has been a long and odd day."

She looked disappointed again. "Oh. Well, all right then. Shall I see you in the morning?"

"I promise," I said.

Difficult as it was, I left her in the library, and hoped that she would forgive me in the fresh light of the sun. I went upstairs to my room and changed into a lightweight wool pants and jacket. I grabbed a hat and looked in the mirror. Same old Reggie.

"Pelham," I said. "Let's go for a walk."

And so it was that for the second night in a row I found myself trailed by Pelham as I walked into the woods just after 8:30 p.m. We avoided policemen at the main doors by taking Mimsy's suggestion and exiting through the side door past the conservatory. This door was mainly used by servants, and it was also near to a set of French doors on the same side of the house that opened off of the library. Instead of posting two constables within such close proximity, the Chief Inspector had placed a single man between the doors. It was a simple matter to slip out under cover of darkness and wait for him to look the other way before nipping around in the opposite direction. I felt quite like a cat burglar. Except feline wasn't the order of the day, really.

I had assiduously avoided any discussion of why we might be out walking in the woods at night. The last thing I wanted to do was hear Pelham drone on about peasant superstition. The whole ruddy business had me so anxious that I thought nothing of using a word like "assiduous." I tried to whistle a tune as I sauntered, but it was as if my mouth was full of crackers. Pelham seemed grimly efficient, which quite frankly is how he usually seems. Dealing with this werewolf business had no more effect on him than if I'd asked him to press my trousers or air the best bedroom. I wondered where he got his training. I'm sure I must have known at some point, but one does have so much to keep track of.

Upon reaching the clearing, however, it became clear things would need discussing. I had no romantic rendezvous planned on which to blame the woodsy foray; it was clear to both me and Pelham why I had brought us out here. Added to this was the rather uncomfortable fact that as we walked towards the clearing—a good three hundred yards through the trees south of the lawn—I began to feel decidedly strange. It would soon become necessary to speak.

"Pelham," I said. "I feel I must admit I have brought you here not only for the purpose of taking the air."

"I deduced as much, sir."

"You are, as always, astute, my good man."

"Perhaps it is the atmosphere of investigation under which we've spent the day. At all events, I understood your desire to go for a walk as being intimately connected with our discussion of the moon and its effects immediately prior to dinner."

"Just so, Pelham. Just so. And now I wonder if you'd be so good as to advise me. I seem to be feeling quite odd."

"In what way, sir?"

"I am somewhat muddle-headed and there is a sense of

vagueness which I am at a loss to credit. Perhaps the most obvious sensation I'm experiencing at the very moment is that my skin feels tight."

"Your skin, sir?"

"Honestly, Pelham, there are times when you seem quite deaf. My skin feels tight, as if it were a pair of Fitchly Skorjenhensen's trousers. I feel as if I'm about to burst right out of myself."

"It is likely, sir, that you are. If I may make a suggestion?"

"Yes, Pelham?" I had begun to sweat at this point, though the night could be properly characterized as mild.

"I would suggest you remove your clothing, sir."

"Pelham!"

"It is only to prevent my disposing of their remnants later, which would undoubtedly be the case otherwise. If your modesty is offended, I shall avert my gaze." Realizing the wisdom of this rather indecorous suggestion, I began to disrobe, handing each piece of my ensemble to Pelham as I did so. I can't express the oddness of the whole situation. Though I suppose I just did.

"Pelham, I'm just a tad terrified."

"Indeed, sir. I can reassure you I will remain vigilant for your safe return in the morning, and will be here to provide you with clothing and any other necessaries."

"You're a good man, Pelham. I was rather more worried about the evening itself. I've never been a wolf, you see."

"We can only hope for the best, sir. I do not know what to expect, nor do I present myself as an expert on werewolves. If it is any consolation to you, sir, I have always had the utmost confidence in your ability to handle whatever life lays in your path."

This amounted to a testimony of undying love from a man of Pelham's reserved nature. I very nearly grasped his shoulder in an outpouring of manly affection. I refrained, because I was naked. Then a horrible thought occurred to me.

"Good lord, Pelham. Should you be here? What if . . . what if I eat you?"

"I appreciate your concern, sir. I feel quite safe. I feel it unlikely you will attack me, and I feel I can adequately handle myself on the remote chance that you do."

"How can you be so certain, Pelham? You say you've never encountered a werewolf before."

"Well, I did acquit myself admirably yesterday evening, sir. And though I have limited experience of werewolves, I have seen and occasionally engaged in physical altercations with other supernatural creatures."

"Such as?"

"The most difficult encounter of that kind in my experience was with an Egyptian beetle-creature which haunted London near the turn of the century. I was young and impetuous, and unaware of the dangers of the hypnotic powers of the Priestesses of Isis."

"Pelham, I suspect you omitted several important bits of information from your résumé when you applied for employment with me."

"I included what I felt to be relevant experience, sir. I had no foreknowledge you would become a werewolf."

"Fair enough, old man."

And then the moon rose. Neither Pelham nor I could see it yet, due to the trees around us which blocked the horizon. There was no increase in the light; the near-total darkness of the clearing held sway. But I could *feel* the deuced thing, somehow just knew the rim of the moon had peeked above the edge of the earth. And, along with the rising of the moon, it happened.

It is a task, dear reader, to adequately express the transformation of man to wolf. Even now, when I have experienced the change dozens of times, it still seems a rum thing. Trust me, when I say you can't understand it unless you've done it, that cliché has never had such forceful ties to reality. I can safely and accurately employ phrases like "elongation of vestigial tail" or "face thrust forward, stretching impossibly into a muzzle" or "rapid and substantial growth of coarse grayish hair or fur over all parts of my body," but those phrases would not completely convey the meaning I intend. Even "nauseating cracking as my bones lengthened and realigned" doesn't quite capture it.

At any rate, those descriptions don't at all address what seems to me an even more important aspect of werewolfery. Or if less important, only slightly so. Dear reader, I deal now with minutiae. Trust me that what I'm about to discuss is pretty bloody important.

The mind changes as well, you see. One does not become completely unaware of what is happening; in fact I was at times too much aware. But the wolf nature does tend to dominate, as it were, and it is difficult to the point of what-have-you to try and resist. The result is that I have some recollection of the evening's events between moonrise and dawn, but in the heat of the moment, if you will, I had very little input into the whats and wheres. It was not, I must stress, the same as being along for the ride while my wolfish body did things I had little control over. But it was as near as dash it.

According to Pelham's later report, the whole process took something less than two minutes. I can't say it was terribly painful, or even that it was the worst thing I've ever gone through. But, if I began to list aloud all the experiences I've ever had, beginning with the most pleasurable and working my way down to excruciatingly horrible, you could certainly go have a sandwich and a bit of a lie down and feel safe you could return before I said "turning into a wolf." Interspecies transitions, I mean to say.

Pelham tells me I ran off into the woods without a backward glance. I'm glad I didn't attack and kill Pelham, at least, because there is little I have less tolerance for than ingratitude. I had no thoughts for Pelham at all, and I worried not a jot about murderers or blackmail or the softness of Mimsy Borogove's lips. My first night as a wolf had begun.

Chapter Nine

I thought perhaps I could do a rather terrifying collage here. You know the sort of thing I mean:

A swirling rush of leaves and underbrush. I lunge through the trees, governed only by the whims of the full moon and the animal urges within me.

But that would be disingenuous of me, and I have too much respect for you, dear reader, to engage in such tactics. I have only vague recollections of much of the night, but I firmly believe I spent the first hour or so mainly running through the woods, sniffing at anything I could get my snout on, and peeing on trees. I can say with some authority that peeing on a tree is a far more enjoyable experience than one might expect. I don't know I ever gave the subject much thought prior to that weekend at Huffsworthy Hall, but the thing was a revelation. Quite satisfying.

A wolf has no intense desire to maim or kill people or other animals unless provoked somehow. A hungry wolf will kill to eat, something which I did not do that first evening, but will not attack a person for that purpose, unless literally starving and having nothing else at hand. Luckily, I had dined only a few hours earlier, and even though I had not supped hugely (I was, you may remember, suspicious of Dobbins' cooking), I was not hungry. I believe the word for what I did is "romp." I romped with lycanthropic abandon. I picked up sticks and tossed them; I rolled in leaves and various bits of offal; I chased rabbits for fun; I drank from freshly flowing streams. And, as I said, there was much peeing.

Wolves do tend to be suspicious of other wolves, if they are not of their own pack. So it was that the central event of the evening, or at least the one which remains in my mind with somewhat more clarity than the rest, occurred somewhere in the woods southeast of the clearing from which I had initially run. I was trotting rather contentedly through the oaks and what-not when I caught the tantalizingly familiar whiff of something else close by. A moment later I rounded a particularly protuberant shrub and found myself face to face with the wolf that had bitten me the night before.

I would have recognized the bally thing anywhere, but the smell was a dead giveaway. It was a large gray wolf, much like myself, but with a bit lighter color coat. It was standing by a little stream facing me. Its head was lowered, its hackles raised, and it was growling. Now, I may have been new to this wolf business, but I can read body language like I was born to it. I could also, I discovered, growl with the best of them. I was still enjoying the low rough feel of the growl when the ruddy beast leapt, for the second time in twenty-four hours, for my throat.

I must say I was much better equipped to meet the challenge this time. Indeed, I began to see decided advantages to being a wolf as I dodged the initial lunge and reciprocated by nipping the thing on the ear. We rolled and scuffled a bit, neither of us laying paw or tooth on the other to any real extent, and then splashed into the edge of the stream, barking and growling for all we were worth. I regret the loss of civilized conversation while being wolfy, but I found we could get our points across in a fair manner. I was the larger wolf, and thus had the advantage. What a difference a species makes—the beastie had seemed impossibly huge the night before, when I was a mere picnicking lover. Now, with the odds skewed slightly in my favor, I let my newly found instincts take over, and hey presto!

Eventually I landed a blow to end the skirmish, if I might employ so military a term. I was able to get in a really solid gashing bite on the other wolf's back right leg, at which act I felt blood rush into my mouth and heard the satisfying yelp of the cursed animal. I fell back into the stream and the other wolf dashed off, clearly aware who had the better of this bout, most likely to quite literally lick its wounds.

In the way of wolves, I suppose, I didn't spend much time being concerned about this violent encounter. I drank from the stream, caught my breath somewhat, peed on a tree, and wandered off in another direction. There is a freedom in the sort of in-the-moment thinking that characterizes the wolf. No regrets for the past, no real anxiety for the future. Luckily I have been trying to cultivate such an approach to life for some time, or else the shift may have disoriented me somewhat. The rest of the evening was what could be accurately called uneventful. At any rate, I remember only flashes of rather uninteresting but frightfully fun romping until morning.

The morning brought with it another host of developments. There was a blank period wherein I remember nothing at all, and then there were birds singing and the thin light of early morning dimly illuminating the clearing, to which I had returned. I awoke to a pleasant feeling of contentment, and a joy sprung from a conviction that all was right with the world. I stretched, yawned, smacked the lips, and looked around. I was astonished at how good I felt. Very quickly, however, I began to notice aspects of the morning which weren't composed of unmitigated joy.

For one thing, I was rather chilly as I lay in the dewy grass. For another, I was most likely cold because I was stark naked. For a third, there was no sign of Pelham, who had promised to meet me with clothes and post-lupine comfort. Perhaps it was too early. I stepped into the trees, in the unlikely case of someone other than Pelham coming into the clearing, and waited. I was now quite cold and in need of a lavatory. The trees looked decidedly less attractive for this purpose in the morning light.

After what seemed a longish time standing behind a beech tree and watching the sunlight increase in the clearing, I finally had to admit the uncomfortable possibility that Pelham was not coming. I looked around for anything with which to shield my vulnerability, and could find nary a fig leaf, actual or metaphorical.

So, hands cupped politely near the areas of my anatomy least acceptable to polite society, I began to make my way houseward. I had no idea what could have kept Pelham, but I was keen to have a word or two.

I picked my way rather tenderly through the trees and outlying grounds, making it as far as the stables before I heard voices. I hid myself behind a barrel of oats or some such grainy feed to watch for the clearing of the coast, but as I sat there no one seemed in evidence. I listened carefully, still wolfy in the ears you understand, and realized the murmuring voices were coming from inside the stables. I felt keenly the need to find something to render me unnude, but was moved by some instinct to snoop. Stretching up on my toes, I could just peer through a window into the stables. I had no real preconceived notions as to who would be in the Huffsworthy stables at 6 a.m., but not even had you put my head in a set of forceps and commanded me to guess would I have contrived to express the scene that lay before me.

Fitchly Skorjenhensen and Arabella Biscuit were in the stables. Arabella was sitting on a hay bale, buttoning a blouse I had not seen her wear before, and Fitchly was standing by the stalls with his back to her, petting Abercrombie. The most disturbing part of the whole ruddy thing was Arabella's appearance. She was positively disheveled. Her hair was wildly uncombed and had stray bits of straw protruding from it, and her face and chest were flushed with exertion.

She finished dressing and called to the big Swede. "I'm ready, Fitchly."

Skorjenhensen turned and crossed to her. He bent down and swept her up in his arms, and Arabella laid her head on his shoulder and sighed. They moved towards the door.

I sat back down behind my barrel with no idea how to react. I could not believe what I had seen, though I had no choice, even though believing is the last thing I would have done but for the evidence of my eyes. Arabella and Fitchly! How could I break the news to Moony? I was deeply and truly shocked—Arabella had seemed so entwined with Moony in the garden yesterday, and Fitchly had been vehement in his disavowal of Arabella. I had wanted to discount what I had witnessed in the dining room, but this was a different kettle of half-dressed fish. The world had gone mad.

After giving the unlikely couple a chance to be completely out of range, I moved crouchingly out from behind the barrel and began moving through the gardens towards the side door through which Pelham and I had made our previous evening's exit. I was becoming extremely anxious as the sun got higher. I could certainly do nothing about this new and nauseating turn of events until I found my way into the house and got on some clothes. I was pondering just how to do this, when I came around the corner of the house and ran into a policeman.

Now, I can't say for certain whether you've ever tried to explain to a police constable why you're trying to get into a house at 6:30 a.m. while you are naked. I will say nudity is a deterrent to success in most conversations with members of a rural police force, and this was no exception. I felt extremely visible. Neither of us spoke for nearly fifteen seconds. The constable was one whom I hadn't seen before. He looked perplexed and embarrassed, and I had time to feel sorry for putting him in the situation before Pelham arrived. For even while I was still attempting to formulate my thoughts, Pelham stepped out of the house through the door I had been making for. He had a shirt and pair of trousers from my closet, and he looked as deucedly efficient as ever.

"Ah, Mr. Spiffington," he said, "I am very happy to find you here." He handed me the clothes, and I was not remiss in swiftly stepping into them. The constable turned to Pelham and vented his consternation.

"You can vouch for this person, sir?" he asked of my valet.

"Indeed, constable. This is Mr. Reginald Spiffington of Regent's Park, London, a guest of Lord Huffsworthy."

"Is it indeed? And does Mr. Reginald Spiffington make a habit of wandering the garden of a morning in his altogether?"

Pelham lowered his voice to a conspiratorial murmur. "You'll have to excuse my employer, Constable Wiggins. Mr. Spiffington is unfortunately rather fond of scotch, and I'm afraid that when under its influence he often feels the convention of clothing somewhat too confining. It is something his family have often spoken to him about."

The constable looked at me. "Sir? Do you drink?"

I looked at Pelham and then back at Constable Wiggins, my belt still dangling. I swallowed. "Like a fish," I said.

Forty minutes later I had bathed and shaved, and was just finishing the redressing as Pelham explained again how difficult it was to get out of the house early in the morning with the police at every door. "It is exceedingly hard," he was saying, "to explain why I would need to go into the garden with a suit of clothes over my arm before six in the morning."

"It is exceedingly hard," I said, "to wander unsuited through the grounds of Huffsworthy Hall at dawn." This was what is generally referred to as a retort. "I wish you hadn't told the constable I had been drinking."

"It was the only plausible explanation, sir. It would perhaps have been prudent for you to remain where you were."

"Perhaps, Pelham, perhaps. But what is prudence to a man who has been as one with his animal nature? I was, shall we say, wolfishly impetuous."

"Yes, sir. You seem to have come through the evening in good form."

"Indeed I did, Pelham. It was quite an experience." I told him about the events of the evening as well as I could remember them, and then revealed the startling scene I had witnessed in the stable earlier that morning. He was satisfyingly shocked.

"I find it difficult to credit Miss Biscuit in an assignation with Mr. Skorjenhensen," he said. "Are you absolutely certain?"

"Well, they weren't exactly *in flagrante delectable*, but close enough for my money. Her hair was a mess, and she was half-dressed. It was considerably closer to an assignation than I've ever seen her with Moony."

"Does that alter your perception of the events of yesterday?"

"You mean the murder? I'm dashed if I know, Pelham. It doesn't materially affect the Huffsworthy/Dobbins angle, but it does mean that Fitchly was lying to us yesterday afternoon. And I wonder why he would?"

"Presumably to keep their relationship from reaching the ears of young Mr. Huffsworthy."

"Perhaps, Pelham, perhaps. But then I don't see why she would act like she was interested in Moony in the first place. I suppose it could have been a way to get under her father's skin, but the old prune's gone now—no reason to keep it up. Blast it all, she seemed so ruddy sincere!"

"Indeed, sir. I believed her interest in Mr. Huffsworthy to be genuine."

"Then, crumbs, Pelham, I don't know."

"Nor do I, sir. And nothing in your encounter with the other wolf gave a clue as to its identity?"

"Well, no. It was a bloody great wolf. There were no distinguishing marks. But I gave it something to think about, what? That was no slight wound I gave the ruddy thing."

"Sir, if your bite was as deep as you indicate, it is possible that the werewolf may give itself away this morning."

"But we heal like gangbusters, don't we? My arm was better by breakfast."

"Yes, sir. But your wound, though not insubstantial, was not terribly deep. And even it was still evident for several hours the next morning. A bite like the one you describe would surely still be in evidence for at least part of the day. We should monitor the gait of others."

"I shall endeavor to do so, Pelham. Now, it must be nearly 8:00 a.m. We should be thinking about breakfast."

Chapter Ten

It was, actually, after eight. I was the last to arrive at the table, and therefore had no chance to see the others walk in. As I sat there, smelling the bacon a-sizzle in the pan, I looked at each of the others in turn. None of them looked like the wolf I had tussled with the night before, but then I suppose I had also lost the canine aspect. Mimsy was a bit cool to me at first, but seemed to soften when I flashed the pearlies. Arabella was all attention to Moony, and Fitchly sat across from them, seemingly neither interested nor concerned. Things were getting a little overwhelming, to tell the honest. I mean to say: a murderer amongst us, a werewolf amongst us, Arabella and Moony, Arabella and Fitchly, blackmail, poison, European art songs, and policemen getting a good long look at my John Thomas. And that doesn't even consider my own lupine persona, a development which I had scarcely time to consider in its long-lasting effects. I could hardly concentrate on my kippers, though I do remember the eggs being done to a nicety.

But if I had thought to get through a meal without incident at the Huffsworthy table, I was to be plunged into the depths of disappointment, having only myself to blame for expecting something so clearly without precedent. I had only just started my second cup of tea when Detective Inspector Mutton entered the room, walked directly to Mimsy Borogove, and bent down to whisper in her ear. As the man's whisper was like unto a steam pipe in an echo chamber, I can accurately report his words to her.

"We need to see you in the library, Miss." Mimsy looked confusedly at the Inspector, then confusedly at me, and then napkined her lovely lips and stood to follow him. I did the same.

"Now, there's no need for anyone but Miss Borogove," said Mutton.

"No, I'd like Reggie to come," said Mimsy.

Other guests had stood up by this point. Lord Huffsworthy spoke. "If there is a development in the investigation, perhaps we should all?"

"No, no, no. This isn't the way we want to go about it at all." Mutton faced us in the doorway, his mustaches aquiver. "This is outside the norm to a high degree. We only want Miss Borogove."

"Are we not allowed to come along?" I asked.

"I'd just rather you not," said Mutton uncomfortably.

"Are we," Lord Huffsworthy asked, "legally prevented from accompanying you?"

"Well, no," said Mutton. "You're not 'legally prevented.' But we would rather—"

"Then we'd like to hear," squeaked Arabella. "If you've got information about my father's murder, we deserve to know. I do at least." Moony squeezed her arm in support, and she smiled weakly up at him.

Mutton turned and led the way into the library, grumbling under his mustaches.

Chief Inspector Pail was not best pleased to see us all. "I told you to bring Miss Borogove, and we'd do this nice and quiet like," he said to Mutton in an undertone.

"I told 'em, Chief Inspector," returned Mutton at the same volume. "I told 'em. There was no stopping 'em. The whole lot of 'em *would* come."

"Just what's all this then?" Pail asked us.

I said, "What do you want with Mimsy?" and the floodgates opened. Everyone clamored for answers, wanting to know what had been discovered, whether the doctor's report had been made, if there were any leads, etc. Pail held out his hands and made tamping motions. "Now, now, now, now! Let's just have a bit of calm and I'll tell you what there is to be told." We quieted down. He clearly enjoyed the effect. Once we had settled down, Pail sent Mutton out of the room with a direct-to-ear murmur that even my sharpened ears missed. "Now, here," he said, "is how it stands." He placed his hands behind his back like a politician.

"We have gotten the doctor's report, and it looks like Sir Lionel was poisoned to death."

"I told you as much," said Mimsy.

Pail looked at her and said slowly, "Why, yes, you did, Miss Borogove. You certainly did. We also did a search of the body and discovered something. We discovered the very something that Detective Inspector Mutton is bringing in even as we speak!"

We waited. Detective Inspector Mutton did not appear.

"Was it a piece of evidence?" asked Moony. Pail held up a forefinger.

"Ah, ah, ah!" he said. "Just half a moment, Mr. Huffsworthy." We waited another six minutes or so in silence, our sporadic attempts to ask questions cut off by Pail's impressive and forceful hand gestures. I finally sat down and began leafing through a copy of *A Shropshire Lad*.

Eventually Mutton returned with a deep wooden box held twixt his sirloin-like hands. I closed my book and stood next to Mimsy. After some muttering between the two Inspectors, Chief Inspector Pail faced us again.

"Thank you for your patience, my good people. I was saying, before our rather overlong pause . . . " here he shot a glance at Mutton.

"It was way out in the car!" muttered Mutton.

" . . . I was saying we had discovered something on Sir Lionel's body. What we discovered was this!" And with a flourish, Pail waved his hand at Mutton, who, with a similar flourish, pulled from the box Mimsy's manuscript.

Mimsy gasped. "Ah-ha! I knew the little man had stolen my book!"

Pail looked at her again with that slow deliberate stare. "Did you indeed, Miss Borogove?" he asked.

Mimsy's demeanor changed. She moved from adorably indignant to being adorably wary. "What are you implying, Inspector?" she said.

"Did you know that digitalis, which is what the doctor seems to think was the poison that killed Sir Lionel, is often found in a common flower garden, Miss Borogove?"

"Here, now, what is going on?" asked Lord Huffsworthy.

"I'd like to know if Miss Borogove is aware of digitalis' life as a flowery ornamental," said Pail. "Miss Borogove?"

"Yes, I know that," she said. "Digitalis is the flower foxglove. That's fairly common knowledge, Inspector."

"I admit that wasn't a fair question, Miss Borogove. I've read *Salad Days*, where you used foxglove poisoning as your murder weapon."

"I write crime novels, Inspector. I must have a murder weapon in each book."

"It is Chief Inspector, actually. And I can't fault you for putting a murder in a murder mystery, certainly." He chuckled. "I'm more interested in what Detective Inspector Mutton discovered in your room whilst you were at breakfast." And here he gestured again to Mutton, who reached back into his box of wonder and pulled out the two foxglove flowers I had given Mimsy the previous afternoon. "Are these yours, Miss Borogove?" There was general sense of I-didn't-see-that-coming from the bystanders.

I said, "But I gave—" and Mimsy hit me in the stomach with the flat of her hand.

"Yes, Chief Inspector, those flowers are mine. Surely a woman can have a vase of flowers to brighten up her room?"

Chief Inspector Pail gestured to Mutton, who drew a pair of handcuffs from his pocket. "I'm afraid you'll have to come with us, Miss Borogove."

"Surely you can't be serious!" I said. "This is ludicrous! Lord Huffsworthy, this man is arresting one of your guests. Can you not—!?"

"The Chief Inspector seems to be doing the job for which he

is paid, Mr. Spiffington," said the lord of the manor. "I cannot obstruct the enforcers of our laws."

"Reggie," said Mimsy from within her cuffs. "Reggie, it's all right. I trust you."

"Trust me?"

"I trust you to finish what we've started, darling. I know you'll find the truth."

Detective Inspector Mutton took Mimsy by the elbow and walked her towards the door. As they passed me, Mimsy pulled away from him and pressed her lips to mine. She was pulled rather roughly back.

"Mimsy, I shall." I said. "Or Pelham and I shall. Either way I will exonerate you!"

"Please do," she said. "You're my only hope."

"Come along now, Miss Borogove," said Detective Inspector Mutton. "We've a nice little cell waiting for you." And he walked her out.

Clamor was the order of the hour then. Everyone in the room began talking at once, expressing opinions on Mimsy's arrest, on the poisoning, on the flowers. I needed to leave the room, but most of the room left as well, all of them having, it seemed, the same idea. I pushed my way out behind Moony and Arabella, and to my great relief found Pelham in the hall.

"Pelham! Good god, Pelham, they've arrested Mimsy!"

"So I have surmised, sir," said Pelham. "This is a most unfortunate turn of events."

"And they used the flowers I gave her as evidence."

"Most distressing, sir."

"And she wouldn't let me give the alibi! Surely if the police knew that I had given her the flowers it would take their airtight case and make it, well, a sight less airtight, I'd say."

"Perhaps," said Pelham, "she wanted you to seem unconnected with the immediate business in order to continue your investigations. And surely the most certain way of securing Miss Borogove's timely release from incarceration is to expose the identity of the true murderer."

"Yes, of course. It's only that, well. Investigating seemed to run much more smoothly with Mimsy's assistance."

"I fully understand, sir."

"I'd hate to muck it up, you see."

"I have confidence in you, sir. And I am still available to render whatever assistance you may need."

At that I rallied. "Of course you are! Good man, Pelham. We shall find our way through these darkling plains, though ignorant armies clash in our path, if I may so abuse Tennyson."

"Arnold, sir."

"Yes, Pelham, his first name is not of consequence. The question is what is our next move?"

We were alone in the hallway. Pelham lowered his voice and said, "Perhaps it would be a favorable moment to discuss the other unanswered question at hand, that of the identity of the other werewolf. Were you able, as I was, to observe the other guests as they left the library a moment ago?"

"Crumbs, Pelham, I did not! I was too upset by Mimsy's arrest. Did you see anything helpful?"

"I believe so, sir. There was one person leaving the library just now who was limping badly, as if from an injury to the right leg."

"Really? Pelham that's wonderful! We have our man, then. Who was it?"

"It was Miss Arabella Biscuit."

"Pelham, are you sure?"

"Very sure, sir. You will admit there is no one among those recently gathered in the library who could be reasonably mistaken for Miss Biscuit. She was most definitely limping. She in fact was leaning on Mr. Huffsworthy for support as they moved across the hall."

"I say, Pelham. I wasn't expecting Arabella. The other wolf I clashed with in the woods last night didn't seem like Arabella. It was quite aggressive."

"Miss Biscuit may similarly feel the wolf she met didn't seem like you, sir. But it was."

"It was indeed, Pelham. It was indeed. I suppose that answers the question as to what we do next. I think I need to have a talk with Arabella."

"I would think it not imprudent, sir. And if I may accompany you, sir?"

"Certainly, Pelham. Though I feel I can ask the necessary questions."

"My request to accompany you does not proceed from hesitancy about your investigative abilities, sir. I am interested in the werewolf phenomenon, particularly as I now find myself valet to one. If Miss Biscuit truly is a werewolf, she may provide insight that could prove useful in the future."

"Rather! Pelham, I welcome your company. Let us go."

And so we went. Arabella had left the house with Moony a few moments before, and thus Pelham and I went out into the sunshine to seek her. The day was warming up rapidly, and I found myself reaching for a handkerchief to mop the brow. As we walked, a thought occurred to me.

"Pelham?" I said.

"Yes, sir?"

"Perhaps I misconstrued the scene I witnessed between Arabella and Fitchly Skorjenhensen this morning."

"Indeed, sir?"

I stopped by the corner of the house and faced him. "If Arabella is what we think she is, then I must have. I was coming back to the house after my own transformation. Arabella must have just gone through the same thing."

"Yes, sir, you are most astute. I wonder that it had not yet occurred to me. That would explain her disheveled state."

"And it would explain why Fitchly needed to carry her, because her leg was hurt. Which means . . . crikey, Pelham, that means Fitchly Skorjenhensen knows!"

"Indeed, sir. Well deduced." We began to walk again.

"Then we need to talk with both of them, Pelham. There is something wildly amiss."

"Given the events of the weekend so far, sir, I feel compelled to view that as a marked understatement of the situation."

"Pelham, this deduction business is extremely invigorating. My brain is positively abuzz. This is what kept Sherlock Holmes on the trail, I am sure. The thrill of the unknown! The furious workings of the mind!"

"Perhaps the two are as one for someone such as yourself, sir."

"No, Pelham, I need no accolades. This case is far from closed."

We discovered Arabella and Moony in the garden, walking hand in hand near the same bench I had found them on the day before. Arabella had her head on Moony's shoulder, and they were all-in-all quite chummy and slightly nauseating.

"Arabella," I said, "Pelham and I would like to talk with you in the library, if we could."

Moony said, "Reggie. We both feel awful about Mimsy. Are you okay, old man?"

"I am fine, Moony, partially because I am certain Mimsy is innocent. But at this moment I do need to talk with Arabella, if you could spare her."

"I think Arabella has been through quite a lot these last two days, Reggie."

"Arabella, could I speak with you briefly? I know you have suffered these last few days, and I promise not to keep you long."

Arabella looked at Moony and then at me. "Could we not talk here, Mr. Spiffington?" she asked. "It is very pleasant in the garden, and there is nothing you could have to say to me that you cannot say in front of Archibald."

"Really? I mean, are you sure? I want to talk to you about the little stream in the woods south of here, and about the state of the stables in the early morning hours."

She went paler, an effect not unlike chalking a slab of alabaster. "Oh. Perhaps we should adjourn to the library, Mr. Spiffington."

"What? Arabella, what's this about?" Moony looked incredulous.

"It won't take long, darling," said Arabella, putting her hand against Moony's cheek. "Just a moment or two. I promise to explain everything to you afterwards."

We left the garden together, leaving Moony looking forlorn and confused in our wake. Arabella Biscuit was silent as we walked back to the house. She was still limping slightly, though even in the short time since Mimsy's arrest her leg seemed to have improved over what Pelham had described. In the library, I asked Arabella to sit on the large sofa under the window, and I took the leather armchair opposite. Pelham stood at my right elbow. I was unsure how to broach such a delicate subject. I believe I actually said, "I suppose you're wondering why I've asked you here?"

Arabella said, "I'd supposed it was to talk about werewolves, Mr. Spiffington."

"Ah. Yes, well, that is what I wanted to talk about."

"You think I am the werewolf that attacked you on Friday evening and that you subsequently met in the woods again last night. You want to know if I am responsible for your becoming a werewolf."

"Ah. Yes, well, those are the questions that first come to mind. I don't suppose it would be prying for me to ask?"

"I should have spoken to you before now, but my fear prevented me. Mr. Spiffington, I owe you so great an apology I can scarcely see how to approach it." She seemed to draw herself up, as much as a Noodle can. "I am indeed a werewolf. I have been for six years, since just after my fifteenth birthday."

"A perverse form of birthday present, one would say," I remarked.

"Yes, Mr. Spiffington, I agree. My present that year was actually a trip to Constantinople—I suppose now they prefer 'Istanbul'—aboard the Orient Express. Typically, my father gave me a gift he could enjoy to the fullest. The train was opulent and luxurious, and our journey was in the height of comfort. Once in Istanbul we traveled into the countryside to stay at a resort in the mountains near the Black Sea. It was beautiful and exotic, and like most things my father did it was extravagant in the extreme."

"It is certainly larger than any birthday gift I ever received," I said.

"I would have preferred a book or a new dress. But I did enjoy the Turkish countryside, the scenery was lovely and the people warm and friendly. But I was still traveling with family. One night after my father had yet again embarrassed me by berating a servant to tears during dinner, I left the hotel and walked out into the moonlight. I was a distraught teenager, and I did not pay attention to my surroundings. I did not see the wolf until I was right upon it. It was feeding on a deer—there was a lot of blood—and I screamed. When I did, it turned and leapt at me, clawed my arm and bit my neck. I nearly bled to death."

"Good god, Arabella. How ever did you survive?"

"My scream saved me. A fisherman who was making his way home near the spot heard me and came to help. He beat the wolf off with a branch, and took me to a doctor. He also told my father and I that the wolf that had attacked me was actually a local potter named Orhan. Of course we thought him a quaint peasant."

"Until the next evening," said Pelham.

"Yes, Mr. Pelham. Until the next evening."

"How did your father react to the change?" asked Pelham. "It is not possible for someone as young as you were to keep such a thing hidden from your parent."

"No, my father certainly knew. He . . . managed my time as a werewolf."

"I say, Arabella, don't cry!" I handed her a handkerchief. Nothing more unsettling than a woman crying. "I know your father's death is still fresh, but we want to do anything we can, you know."

She laughed. "Mr. Spiffington, I don't want to seem cold, but I find it difficult to be upset over my father's death. When I say my father managed my transformations, what I mean is that he acted as zookeeper."

"I'm afraid I don't follow you."

"Just before sunset on the three nights around the full moon, my father would take me into the cellar of our house in Sussex. There was a thick support post that stood near the center of an empty room there, and my father would chain me to it. Then he would leave me until the next morning."

"Good Lord! Arabella, that's horrible! I can't imagine a father treating his child in such a manner, even a child who has become a raging supernatural beast."

"My father was a cruel man capable of many things beyond the imagination of reasonable thinking adults. He felt I had become a freak, and the way one treats freaks and animals is to lock them up so they can't harm anyone else. The bruises you saw on my neck and shoulders were not, as you supposed, the result of my father beating me, but were in fact the abrasions of the chain around my neck."

"Of the chain . . . you mean he chained you up here at Huffsworthy Hall?"

"Oh yes, Mr. Spiffington. He made no exceptions. We normally don't travel during the full moon, but it was important to my father to make Lord Huffsworthy pay his debt. So Friday night he took me into the woods and found a suitable tree, a large oak well away from the house. I removed my clothes, and he chained me up." She reddened with the telling.

"But what happened? Because later I saw—"

"Fitchly happened. For some reason Fitchly was in the woods on Friday night. He burst in upon us just as father was wrapping the chain around my neck."

"He was in the woods because he was following me."

"Really? That makes sense, I suppose. My father would have seen you as a threat to his plans for the weekend because you didn't seem cowed by him. Why were you out in the woods at night?"

"I had, well, you know I was sort of . . . "

"Perhaps we have passed the point of propriety, sir," said Pelham. "Mr. Spiffington had scheduled an evening *tête a tête* with Miss Borogove."

"Oh. That explains some things. Father would not have known that, and so would not have expected Fitchly to be outside at that hour. He didn't want Fitchly to know, you see, because he thought he wouldn't want to marry me if he did."

"I'm surprised someone as conscious of social positions as your father would want you married to a great oaf like Fitchly in the first place," I said.

"That's due to the werewolf business as well, I expect. Father felt I was severely damaged goods, you see. Fitchly was someone he knew could be coerced into keeping quiet once the marriage was in place. And he could keep me close under his thumb." Her eyes were moistening again.

"Miss Biscuit," said Pelham, "to return to the matter at hand, how did Mr. Skorjenhensen react to finding you being chained to a tree by Sir Lionel?"

"Fitchly was perplexed and horrified at first, as anyone would be. I was naked and in chains, with my father standing over me. And then quickly he was furious, as Fitchly often is. He's a strange creature, Fitchly Skorjenhensen. He is as brutal toward his fellow man as is possible, but very gentle and soft-hearted when it comes to animals, as you've seen. Perhaps he connected what he saw with dogs being chained up, something which he abhors. Or perhaps he does have some sort of affection for me." She smiled a small smile. "He knocked my father to the ground, and unchained me. My father began yelling obscenities at him and hitting him in the face with an oak branch. They scuffled, and Fitchly of course very quickly got the better of Father, and took the branch from him. But then—"

"Then," said Pelham, "the moon rose."

Arabella inclined her head. "Just so, Mr. Pelham. The moon rose. And Fitchly saw . . . saw what happens to me when the moon is full."

There was a silence. I hate a silence. I said, "And . . . he was . . . surprised?"

"I don't know from direct experience, Mr. Spiffington, because I was a wolf. I think 'surprise' would constitute a mild description of any sane person's response to what happens to us, don't you?"

"Ah. Well, yes."

"I do know Fitchly tried to catch me. His first rather bizarre instinct was to grab me while I was still recovering from the change, before I had a chance to run. How he escaped being bitten I don't know. I scratched him I think, and he dropped me. I ran off in a rage, and I'm afraid that's when I came upon you."

"I apologize for not recognizing you," I said. She did not seem in the mood for the Spiffington wit, however.

"I am the one who should apologize, Mr. Spiffington. I have only the dimmest memory of our encounter, but I can imagine it was terrifying for you. And the result. Well, I wish there were some way I could truly make recompense."

"Oh, don't mention it, Arabella," I said rather reflexively. "We all make mistakes, and we all have our burdens."

Arabella looked at me seriously. "Mr. Spiffington, I have,

however inadvertently, condemned you to a lifetime of fear and subterfuge, a never-ending cycle of unholy bestial metamorphosis. Your life will be governed by this dark secret for evermore."

"Well. When you put it that way."

"Mr. Spiffington, every aspect of my life is touched by this curse. I would not for the world have passed it on to you or anyone else." She looked likely to cry again.

"I'm sure Mr. Spiffington bears no ill-will toward you, Miss Biscuit," said Pelham. "It is obvious you had no control over your actions."

"Oh, of course!" I added. "Arabella, you're not responsible at all. I blame you not a jot. But I am still curious about one aspect of this whole rum situation."

"I cannot imagine anything I would be loath to share with you at this point, Mr. Spiffington."

"Why was Fitchly Skorjenhensen carrying you back to the house this morning? Was he not so horrified as one might imagine by your wolfish nature? I would have run screaming for the hills, you see. No offense intended, being myself now similarly affected."

"He was quite horrified. He could hardly look at me yesterday morning. But after Father, after they discovered Father, he came to me and asked if anyone else knew. You walked in on the end of our discussion. I told him only he and I now knew, and he was concerned about who would take care of me. I do not think," she added, "that he feels anything but repulsion toward me as a person, but I now rate as an animal —the only things which elicit tender feelings from Fitchly Skorjenhensen. He feared I would be shot or trapped, and so made sure I was well away from the house at moonrise. He also met me at the stables afterwards to bring me clothes, which was fortunate since I was injured."

"My apologies," I said.

"It is nearly impossible to control our actions when we are thus, Mr. Spiffington. We are wolves. If you bear me no ill will for spreading my infection, then I can certainly not chastise you for being in thrall to instinct."

"That's very kind of you, Arabella. And I'm sure to have scads of questions about this 'curse,' as you call it, once we have ascertained the answer to the other pertinent question at hand: who killed your father? And since he wasn't mauled to death in the night, we can safely strike us off the list."

"You will forgive my asking, Mr. Spiffington, but are you are sure the police are mistaken?"

"I am quite sure, Miss Biscuit," I said stiffly. "Mimsy Borogove is the finest of ladies, absolutely above reproach. You can be sure, as I am, that she is not responsible for your father's death."

"Then who did?" asked Arabella.

I looked uncomfortably at Pelham. "I think it's time to visit Dobbins again."

Chapter Eleven

Unfortunately, I was unable to go straightaway to Dobbins. It was by this time within half an hour of lunch, and Dobbins was not accessible. I went to Mimsy's room and handed a ten-pound note to the constable stationed outside her door. Inside I gathered her writing materials—pens, ink, extra nibs, paper, her portable typewriter—and some basic toiletries and packed them in a valise to be sent to Mimsy at the local jailhouse. I had Pelham send this off with one of the constables who was on his way there. The police were in general clearing off; now that the "murderer" had been caught there was little to keep them. The one outside Mimsy's door was only there as a matter of course while her room was still a site of investigation. Pail still puttered around, making notes and finishing paperwork, but even he seemed positively cheery. The case, it seemed, was closed.

Lunch was served on the south veranda overlooking the Duke of Wellington fountain, with the gardens off to the left. I could smell the blooms from here, as well as brief pungent whiffs of stable from around the back of the house. The fare was typical Dobbins: a creamed salmon salad served in lightly browned crêpes with fresh fruit and strawberry champagne. The empty plates from the first course had been removed and we were anticipating the main dish when Lord Huffsworthy raised his glass.

"A toast," he said, "to a most welcome restoration of peace. I'm sure we can all rest easier now that the threat to our safety has been removed." He ostentatiously quaffed his drink, and others at the table did as well, though in a noticeably more subdued and dare I say embarrassed manner. But not Reginald Spiffington, dear reader. I placed my glass back on the linen with a marked and unmistakable forcefulness, such that I may have sloshed the cutlery.

"I am not sure, your Lordship," I said with dignity, "that I have the pleasure of understanding you."

His Not-So-Doleful-As-Previously Lordship met my gaze. "I express my satisfaction that the killer has been apprehended, Mr. Spiffington. I wonder you do not do the same." He looked meaningfully at my glass, standing in a spreading champagne stain.

"I haven't the stomach for toasting miscarriages of justice, your Lordship," I said, and I felt the dander once again on the rise. It had been a weekend for high dander, and this set a new record. "Are you certain your satisfaction does not stem from the lifting of your own anxiety?"

"I beg your pardon, Mr. Spiffington?"

"I only mean to say. Surely it must come as a relief to you that Sir Lionel cannot claim the debt you owed him. Losing a chef would be a great blow. How lovely that you no longer have to concern yourself with this."

Lord Huffsworthy regarded me with shock, his face slowly going purple. "Mr. Spiffington," he said, "you tread on dangerous ground, sir."

"Well, clearly. Anything or anyone on the manor grounds might apparently at any moment be placed as collateral to cover gambling debts. I shouldn't wonder but that we're all on dangerous grounds." I was rather proud of this. A pun, what?

Lord Huffsworthy appeared close to what I assume apoplexy must look like. Purplish face, protruding eyes, small choking noises coming from the throat area. He threw his napkin rather brutally onto the table and said, "How *dare* you, sir? You horrible little rat! You ne'er-do-well! You scurrilous hanger-on! Have you no shame? Is it not enough for you to leech onto my hospitality?"

I felt myself buoyed by my passion for Mimsy Borogove. "Apparently, your Lordship, it is not." And with that, I took three strawberries and a muffin from the table and left the veranda by the French doors into the dining room.

Lord Huffsworthy followed and caught me before I could exit the room. "Mr. Spiffington," he said from the doorway, "am I to understand that you are accusing me of murdering one of my own guests? Those are serious, serious accusations, sir!"

"Lord Huffsworthy, I am not accusing you of murdering Sir Lionel. I only know that Mimsy Borogove is innocent, and that of everyone here, you and Dobbins have the strongest motive."

"I did not poison Sir Lionel Biscuit," said his Lordship. "I readily admit to hating the man. I'll even go so far as to acknowledge it was in my best interests that he be put out of the way. I was at a loss as to how to come to grips with the object of Sir Lionel's visit this weekend. But, painful as it would have been to lose a loyal servant to a grasping peasant like Lionel Biscuit, I would surely have done so if it came to it. I would never stoop to murder."

"Not even to avoid the shame of having your gambling made public?"

"You have just made that aspect of my character public, at least among the guests here, and I have not murdered you."

"Ah, well, the day is yet young, your Lordship. But I see your point."

"You cannot idly toss accusations of this sort around, Mr. Spiffington. I will not have it."

"I cannot let Miss Borogove pay for a crime she did not commit, Lord Huffsworthy. If the police will not find the true killer, then I am obliged to do it for them. Now if you'll excuse me."

"I will not have it, Mr. Spiffington. I am telling you directly to cease making accusations. You are not the police; you have no authority here. You will not inconvenience my guests. If you do not desist from poking your nose where it is not wanted, I will have to ask you to leave. Am I clear, Mr. Spiffington?"

"Yes, I understand you, Lord Huffsworthy."

"Good. Enjoy the rest of your day, Mr. Spiffington." But he didn't really deliver the sentiment behind those words. Truth be told, I cannot say with certainty that Lord Huffsworthy actually desired me to enjoy the rest of my day. He went back out onto the veranda, pulling the French doors rather rattlingly closed behind him. I went through the dining room and into the kitchen.

Now, I am aware I may seem at this point in my narrative to be walking beyond the pale, given my host's emphatic statements. But Reginald Spiffington is not easily cowed. Well, perhaps that isn't one hundred per cent true. Actually, I suppose it would be more accurate to say that Reginald Spiffington is easily cowed. It was very unlike me to stand up to someone like Lord Huffsworthy, who I had lived in mortal terror of since first meeting him during the Christmas vacation my second year at Cambridge. I had come to spend the holidays with Moony, and his father had taken one look at me and declared the nation's moral fiber was eroding. He had gone on to threaten me with a poker for sitting too near the Christmas tree. Moony had told me his father was eccentric, but I found this explanation less than reassuring. The subsequent years had done nothing to assuage my baseline misgivings about Lord Huffsworthy, and even though I had been a frequent visitor to the Hall, I lived in awe of the man. But somehow in the face of his Lordship's smug dismissal of Mimsy as a murderer I could not remain spineless. I felt positively spined. And I was convinced, much as it gave me pain in the deepest recesses of my soul to think so, that Dobbins knew something.

The great chef was in his domain, commanding the two undercooks (or whatever they're called) in putting the finishing touches on the dessert, a crème brulée served with raspberry sorbet. He smiled when he saw me, and waved me in.

"Good afternoon, Mr. Spiffington. Do you require something else at table?"

"No, Dobbins, thank you. I wanted in fact to speak with you."

"But you have not finished your meal! You will miss the dessert."

"I think perhaps," I said, lowering my voice to a husky contralto, if that's not something women do, "that I'm not welcome at the table since I all but accused Lord Huffsworthy of murder a moment ago."

Dobbins became quite still for a few seconds and then said, "Why did you do that, Mr. Spiffington?"

"I suppose my etiquette book is somewhat outdated, but I feel when a murder has been committed, it makes sense to accuse those with the strongest motive, or the strongest opportunity. Or both, Dobbins." I paused for effect, and was rewarded.

"Could we speak somewhere less public, Mr. Spiffington?"

Of course we could. I waited while Dobbins made sure the dessert tray was just so, and while he gave final instructions to the sous chef, a round-faced Frenchman named Antoine. Satisfied, Dobbins wiped his hands on the white cloth that hung from his apron and led me into his office, a cigar box of a room dominated by a large desk that overflowed with cookbooks, receipts, and lists of orders for the stocking of the substantial Huffsworthy pantry. He sat behind the desk and gestured me into a chair opposite. He took a cigarette from a desk drawer and lit it with a match that he tossed into a pristine ashtray. Quite formal, quite the ruler of his tasty little kingdom.

"Now, Mr. Spiffington, could you clarify what you just said? I asked for privacy because it sounded like you may be including me in your 'accusations.' You will understand, Mr. Spiffington, that I am a professional, and you are calling not only my character but my art into question."

"Dobbins, I appreciate your indignation, and I assure you I have the utmost respect for you as an artist. In fact, two years ago you created a curried chicken with cashews that has more than once appeared in my dreams. But, someone has been killed. Actually, allow me to rephrase. Someone has been poisoned. Someone has had foxglove put in his food or drink. You are the preparer of food and drink, Dobbins."

"I am the chef, yes. But there is also Antoine, and his assistant Marcus. And for that matter, any number of servants come in and out of the kitchen."

"Yes, but other servants would not know which plate or cup was Sir Lionel's. You personally oversee the preparation and arrangement of the guests' plates, do you not?"

"Mr. Spiffington, the police have already questioned me extensively on this subject. They have not found sufficient evidence to suspect me or my staff. With all due respect, why do you feel you are better equipped to solve crime than the professionals?"

"Because, Dobbins, I know Lord Huffsworthy had put you up as collateral against his gambling debts. And I know Sir Lionel Biscuit was here this weekend to claim you as his own. I am supposing you left that bit of information out when the police spoke with you?"

I had, it seems, supposed rightly. Dobbins dropped his cigarette and took a moment to rescue his trousers from being burned. When he looked up, he seemed at once rattled and steely, if you see what I mean. A steel rattle was he. He said, "If I withheld any information from the police, I can assure you it was in the service of protecting my employer from scandal and rumor. Surely you understand, Mr. Spiffington."

"You would not have minded being chef to Sir Lionel?"

He opened the drawer again to retrieve another cigarette. "I would have minded it very much. You can imagine my years of service here at Huffsworthy Hall have been not only ideal from a professional standpoint, but have induced in me a feeling of loyalty akin to being part of a family. Lord Huffsworthy is no killer, Mr. Spiffington, and there is no reason to soil his family name. You should feel that, if only for the sake of your friend young Mr. Huffsworthy."

"I understand, Dobbins. And I do apologize for casting aspersions on you or your food. I suppose the murder has shaken us all to some degree."

"It certainly has," said Dobbins, drawing heavily on his cigarette, "but we must be careful how wildly we speculate, Mr. Spiffington. Lives hang in the balance."

"Indeed, Dobbins, indeed. I will certainly take better care in the future."

And I left. You may, perhaps, be wondering at my sudden change of tack. My earlier talk of spines was just bluster, you are imagining. But I have not yet told all. It had taken me some time to catch it, because there were strong and conflicting odors wafting within Dobbins' sanctum. But the second time he opened the drawer I caught it definitely. Faint and fading, but unmistakable. The smell of foxglove.

I left the kitchen and went to find Moony. On the way I saw Bugsby the Butler and asked him if he'd be so good as to nip up to my room and ask Pelham to join me in the library. Moony was advantageously already in the library, perched on a leather armchair and staring dreamily at Arabella Biscuit who reclined on the sofa with her hand over her eyes. When Moony saw me, he stood up, indignant.

"Reggie, what the devil do you mean by it? Embarrassing my father in front of his guests! Are you honestly suggesting my father killed Arabella's father? Oh, I'm sorry, my dear." This last to the Noodle, who sat up at Moony's outburst.

"Moony, old bean, I completely understand your reticence to hear what I've got to say."

"He's gone up to his room, absolutely distraught. What do you mean by it?"

"I mean, Moony, to get to the bottom of this mystery and exonerate Miss Borogove, who has been falsely arrested."

He softened. Moony just didn't have the defiant gene. "Oh, Reggie, I know. How awful for you. I feel so guilty being so happy with my Arabella and there you are with your true love wasting away in a country jail cell."

"I say, Moony, 'true love' is a bit fast out of the gate, what? But I am glad you see where I'm coming from. Because I think I know who is directly responsible for Sir Lionel's death."

Arabella stood now as well, and they faced me like a particularly limp cast of *Romeo and Juliet*. "Who?" asked Arabella. So I told them. Sort of. I told them I had glimpsed a fragment of foxglove in the drawer and that, coupled with Dobbins' demeanor, had been the tip off. Arabella looked a knowing Noodle, and I supposed she guessed closer to the mark. Pelham was correct, as always. Secrets already.

Moony went to see if either Pail or Mutton was still on the grounds. I went to find Pelham, who had taken the car to purchase petrol in preparation for our return journey Monday morning. I found him just returning, and as he put away his driving gear I relayed the new developments to him.

"To be honest, sir, I am not quite surprised. Dobbins is a talented culinary artist, perhaps—"

"Perhaps! Pelham, the gods weep!"

"—but he seems uncouth in his manners when dealing with other servants. I have never held him in any regard."

"Crumbs, Pelham. You've never breathed a breath to me of this. You mean to say all these years you've been harboring a festering how-do-you-mean towards Dobbins?"

"That is a picturesque exaggeration, sir. I did not actively dislike Dobbins, but neither did I feel the warmth of admiration for his character."

"Did?"

"In light of the information you have conveyed, I must revise my earlier opinion of Dobbins. Murdering guests, no matter how unpleasant they may be, is unacceptable behavior in a servant of any rank."

"I suppose you're right, Pelham. Even a chef."

"Even a chef, sir."

"I suppose we should pop down and see if Moony found the Inspector."

We did. And he had. Detective Inspector Mutton was in the library with Moony, awaiting my arrival. He did lots of harrumphing and what's-all-this-then-ing and then had me tell him the whole story from the beginning. Twice. Then he recapped.

"So you think this Dobbins fella is the actual murderer and we have the wrong culprit in the clink at present?"

"Yes, Detective Inspector, that is what I have said several times now."

"Because Sir Lionel was going to take him away from here due to his Lordship's gambling debts."

"Right-o, Detective Inspector. I believe you have it down cold now."

"And you think we should go to the kitchen or servants quarters and find this Dobbins, and I should arrest him."

"I think if he has not succumbed to creeping old age and expired, then that would be an excellent plan, Detective Inspector."

"Well, Mr. Spiffington, I can't say as I thought much of you from the beginning. But if you are right about this, then I will have to congratulate you."

"The cockles of my heart are even now charging up with what passes for warmth, Detective Inspector."

"I said 'if,' Mr. Spiffington. And that 'if' strikes me as a rather large one." He looked around at us all as if he had said something extremely clever. I don't think he had.

"Perhaps we should go and check," I suggested. "I could well be wrong, and then you'd have a laugh, wouldn't you?"

"Mr. Spiffington, I just might. I just might. Let's go and see."

Moony and I left with Detective Inspector Mutton, leaving Pelham behind with Arabella Biscuit. We moved through the dining room and into the kitchen. I had warned Mutton that Dobbins may not be in the kitchen, since there was a lull in the early afternoon before the preparations for dinner began. But I was wrong. Dobbins was in the kitchen. He was slumped across the stove with his face in a saucepan of water. He was stone dead.

Chapter Twelve

As Detective Inspector Mutton said upon initial examination of the body, "No question of bloody poison this time, gents." I'm not a coroner, dear reader, in case you had suspicions to the contrary, but I feel safe in saying Dobbins' death was due in part to a powerful blow to the back of the head. I feel safe in this because there was a heavy frying pan laying on the stove next to the body clotted with blood and hair, and the back of Dobbins' head had been, again quoting the eloquence of the Detective Inspector, "bashed in." Moony turned and leapt for the basin, wherein the poor fellow returned his lunch to the kitchen, and even I had to look away after the initial impression. There was no need to concern ourselves with prolonged exposure, however, as Mutton soon ushered us out of the kitchen with little ceremony and deposited us into the library where we were told to wait.

Pelham and Arabella were still there, waiting for the outcome of our appointment with Dobbins, and I told them of our horrible discovery while Moony sat on an armchair like a piece of chalk in plus fours. Pelham was pensive, if that's not a grammatical term, and expressed himself thusly:

"This is most distressing, sir. I admit to being unprepared for this turn of events."

"Yes, Pelham, I was knocked for six myself. I don't understand it. I thought we had our man."

"It is possible that we did, sir."

"I don't follow you, Pelham. How many murderers do you think went for a weekend in the country this month?"

"I mean, sir, that perhaps Dobbins had been working in tandem with someone else."

"And when the jig was up, the other chap decided to silence Dobbins to prevent it coming to light!"

"Yes, very good, sir. You are reaching Holmesian heights."

"Well, thank you, Pelham. I am achieving a sort of journeyman detective status, what?"

"The question, sir, is who is this villainous cohort?"

"You leap as usual to the heart of things, Pelham. It would be lovely to have the answer to that question."

"But at least there is the positive side of things," said Arabella suddenly.

"We have discovered a second murderer, and are fairly clueless about his or her identity, Miss Biscuit. We are beclouded and I hardly feel the lining is silver. Even plated." I said testily.

"But Mr. Spiffington," she continued, brightly, "don't you see? There is still a murderer at large. Which means the police have *not* locked up a murderer."

A light dawned through the clouds. "Ah-ha! Arabella you are right. Clearly it isn't Mimsy going about the manor house bashing chefs. She *must* be innocent!"

At that moment the rest of the house arrived. Chief Inspector Pail returned, called I imagine by the redoubtable Mutton, and he along with the various constables and other hoo-hahs had herded the house's inhabitants into the library for our second post-murder gathering in two days, not counting the arrest party Pail had thrown that morning. Lord Huffsworthy looked anxious and irritable and clearly had been informed of Dobbins' death ahead of time, unless of course he knew of it through other, more sinister means. I stood near to Arabella and Moony, with Pelham close at hand. I watched each person as they came in. Matilda Nooseheim and the maid staff, which consisted of four waifs of eighteen to twenty-four, all named Jane. Signor Reynaldo MacGregor entered alone, followed by Mr. Smythe, Bugsby, and the male staff. Then Antoine and Marcus came in, looking shocked and pale. They were either very good actors, or else they had no foreknowledge of Dobbins' demise. Fitchly Skorjenhensen, his bruises and scratches still prominent on that broad skull, came sulkily in as well. Pail, flanked by Mutton, addressed us.

"Well, well, well," he said as a placeholder while he looked us judiciously over. "This is quite the place for violent death this weekend, ain't it?" He bounced on his heels a couple of times. "We have confirmed the death of Charles Dobbins, chef to this house, a victim of foul play. Looks like we're back to square one, my good people. Constables at the doors, no one leaving the grounds, the whole shooting match. We'll need to begin questioning each of you again." He sighed. "If you could avoid murdering each other for a couple of days, maybe we could wrap this whole thing up?" He turned to go, but I was quicker than he.

"Chief Inspector?"

Another sigh. "Yes, Mr. Spiffington?"

"You are convinced, I assume that the murderer is still at large?"

"I think it safe to say I've been convinced, Mr. Spiffington. We have a fresh corpse. I'm funny that way."

"But how can that be, Chief Inspector?"

"I think, Mr. Spiffington, if you asked Mr. Dobbins, he would explain how that could be. If he weren't prevented by having had his head bashed in by one of you lot. What part of the situation confuses you, Mr. Spiffington?"

"This morning you were certain you had the murderer behind bars. Lord Huffsworthy seemed fairly convinced of this as well. Surely two men as learned as yourselves were not mistaken?"

The Chief Inspector reddened. Perhaps I was being wolfishly cheeky, but I must admit an element of fun in baiting the little man. He raised his forefinger. "Just you watch it, Mr. Spiffington. That's all."

"Am I to assume Miss Borogove will be released?"

"In light of new information, it is likely Miss Borogove will be released before the end of the day."

"Thank you, Chief Inspector. I merely wondered."

Pail muttered as he left. I caught "cheeky little layabout" and something about a "randy bastard" before he disappeared. Lord Huffsworthy glared at me before following Pail and Mutton. I turned to Pelham, as the others began to filter out of the room.

"Pelham, what do you make of it all?"

"Sir?"

"Well, the murderer must be among us. Who looks likely?"

"I can't say, sir. We must run through the possibilities logically."

"At least," said Arabella, "we can strike Mimsy Borogove off the list. Surely that makes your day brighter, Mr. Spiffington." She and Moony were looking at me with a strange light in their eyes.

"Well, yes," I said, but they continued to stare. They were smiling in a fixed way that unsettled me, and I felt the need to say something.

"I say," I said, "I am unsettled by the fixedness of your smiles. Might I assist either of you with something?"

"You were so forceful just now," said Arabella. "Your love for Mimsy so clearly spurs you onto dangerous ground with no fear of what might befall you."

"Yes, Reggie. Dashed dashing, you know," said Moony.

"Look, that's twice you've come at me with love-talk. Let's just belay that, shall we? Surely it's most important to catch a murderer at this juncture?"

It is most irritating when a female, even a female were-wolf, thinks she knows best. Arabella Biscuit led Moony from the room smilingly. "Of course Reggie," she fired back over her Noodly shoulder, "whatever you say!"

"Pelham," I said, "women, what?"

"As you say, sir."

"You were saying something about logically working through the suspects?"

"Yes, sir. We are not without grounding. Our previous speculations as to motives still apply."

"Lord Huffsworthy?"

"I'm sure I can't say for certain, sir. But it did seem his Lordship had reason to remove Sir Lionel."

"Yes, but. Pelham, that doesn't scan, if you see what I mean.

If Lord Huffsworthy wanted to kill Sir Lionel in order to hang onto Dobbins, doesn't it seem rather uncricket to turn around and kill Dobbins? Bit of a contradiction, what?"

"No, sir. His Lordship feared not the loss of Dobbins, but the exposure of his gambling debts. If he killed Dobbins, it was most likely to prevent Dobbins' knowledge of the first murder coming to light."

"Well, that makes sense."

"Thank you, sir. I try to provide satisfaction."

"Thisa murder," said Reynaldo MacGregor, whom we had forgotten, "itsa not the wolf."

Startled, I turned. "What the devil did you say?"

"I say the wolf, itsa not kill these men."

"No one said they were killed by a wolf. They were poisoned and hit on the head with a skillet. Wolves don't have opposable thumbs, my good man."

Reynaldo MacGregor stepped close. He smelled of linguini and haggis. "There isa *two* wolf here," he said, "but they no kill these men."

"Signor MacGregor, what do you mean?" He started to leave the room, but I caught him by the sleeve. "No, don't slink away, dash it all! You've been wolfing it up all weekend. What do you mean by it?"

"When you ready," he said, "I talka to you. You not ready yet. You come to me later, I help you."

"Help me how? What do you mean?" But he was gone, having somehow slipped his sleeve from my grasp.

"Pelham, what do you make of that?"

"It would seem, sir, that Signor MacGregor has knowledge of the secret you share with Miss Biscuit, and he is offering to give you assistance in some way regarding that secret."

"Honestly, Pelham, I am not entirely dim. How? Why?"

"Answering those questions would lead me into the realm of wild speculation, sir. I am averse to travel there."

"Thank you, Pelham."

Chapter Thirteen

The afternoon was not spent in a way I'd call fruitful. I questioned Matilda Nooseheim, who was thick as a walrus, and discovered that "things is comin' to a frightful head when the cook gets clobbered wif his own pan." I myself was questioned by Chief Inspector Pail, who seemed to doubt my integrity, and who wanted several reiterations of my reasons for suspecting Dobbins in the first place. Since that explanation hinged on a vital piece of information the police had been unable to find out for themselves, the Chief Inspector grew grumpy with each repetition of my story. After ascertaining there was neither motive nor opportunity for my bashing Dobbins, Pail begrudgingly released me back to the wild, where I paced the marble floor of the hallway while Moony watched from a velvet-padded bench next to the telephone table.

"You seem agitated, Reggie."

"I am, as you say, agitated, Moony. I feel the murderous noose tightening around our necks. I want to know who has been killing people this weekend. It is, I daresay, a fair cause for agitation."

"Yes, I suppose so."

"Don't you want to discover the person responsible for killing Arabella's father?"

"Well, yes. But you see, Arabella is so much freer without a father that . . ." He trailed off into a moral swamp.

"Be that as it may, Moony, it's a potential father-in-law dead on the drawing room rug. That can't be good for your own father's reputation."

"I am aware of that, Reggie. I know we should solve the blasted thing."

"And yet, my friend. And yet. I sense a hesitancy born of I know not what."

"I'm worried, Reggie. I'm worried about Daddy."

"About . . . oh. You feel your father is in danger of being accused?"

"You yourself all but accused him at lunch! And if what you say about his gambling debts are true, others will accuse him as well. It's surely much worse for his reputation for him to go to jail."

"Moony, I don't want to insult you. But, is it possible—?"

"That Daddy may have murdered two people in cold blood?"

"Yes."

Moony looked dangerously close to tears. God, I hate when grownish men cry. "I don't know, Reggie. What if he did?"

I didn't have an answer, or at least I didn't have one he could properly appreciate at the moment. The true answer—prison, scandal, ruin—was on the harsh side of brutal given the circs. I simply muttered comforting sounds. This detective business was more difficult than I had supposed. I knew confronting Lord Huffsworthy was something that would most likely be in the offing, and that the police would avoid doing it until every other avenue had been exhausted. Surprisingly, there are drawbacks to the class structure.

Moony went upstairs to find his lady-love. I wondered idly if Arabella would find it in her heart to tell Moony about her monthly problem. I had given no thought at all to how I would deal with this new aspect of my hitherto normal life. For instance, how would I allow for my own monthly problem while in London? Would I now have to leave London every full moon? What about theatre openings and dinners during the season? Just how would my social life be affected by three days of lupine debauchery out of every twenty-eight? I shuddered to think. I had visions of prowling through Soho, frightening pedestrians and leaping after the late-night ladies. Come to think of it, a typical Saturday night.

My beastly reverie was interrupted by Pelham, who came to tell me it was time to prepare for dinner. I wandered bemusedly up to my room and pulled on the tails. Dinner was not awakening anticipation in my mouth or heart, and I was growing irritated that Mimsy had not yet returned from her sojourn in the county facility. I had counted on her being back at the Hall by this point. I wasn't sure how to proceed.

"Pelham, I am not sure how to proceed," I remarked.

"Indeed sir, the situation continues in its opacity."

"I don't think it passable at all. Too many murders, what?"

"Yes, sir. I should have said the answer eludes us."

"It does indeed, Pelham. What we need is a plan worthy of Mimsy Borogove."

"Perhaps Miss Borogove herself could be of assistance?"

"She certainly could, Pelham, but unfortunately Mimsy has not returned from the local jailhouse. A circumstance I intend to inquire into as soon as dinner is over."

"If I may offer, sir?"

"Yes, Pelham?"

"Waiting until Miss Borogove returns suggests itself as the most prudent manner in which to proceed."

"Have you no faith in my powers, Pelham? I did sniff out Dobbins, what?"

"Yes, sir. It may be possible this second murder may not hinge upon olfactory prowess."

"Well, something smells fishy, what?"

"Yes, sir, quite humorous. I only advise caution. The person in question is a violent criminal. He will not volunteer his identity, and may in fact defend it in a dangerous manner, as we have seen in the case of Dobbins."

"I understand, Pelham. I shall be safe as houses."

"Dinner awaits you, sir."

"Thank you, Pelham. I shall go down."

And I went down.

I believe I have already said "dinner was a subdued affair" once in this story, so perhaps the better phrase at this point is "dinner was a rather sad gathering." Antoine had prepared a soup and salad as best he could with the main stove taped off as a crime scene. The food was palatable, and the soup would have been exceptional if I had ordered it at Simpson's, but it did not approach normal expectations for a Dobbinsian meal. The full extent of our culinary loss was clear in the lack of conversation and a general malaise. I suppose the two murders contributed somewhat as well.

Arabella was glancing surreptitiously at Moony, Lord Huffsworthy kept optically shooting dolorous daggers at me, Fitchly Skorjenhensen positively glowered at the entire table, and Signor Reynaldo MacGregor speared his cherry tomatoes with a mysterious yet ultimately forgettable air. I ate a carrot. I was happy at least that the soup contained ham and beef, as I didn't want to go into the night hungry. I thought about Pelham's last words of caution. The murderer wasn't just going to volunteer his identity. Which was a shame really. Much easier that way.

And then, a plan came to me. Fully formed and well-constructed. I felt as Hercule Poirot must, or Holmes himself. It had the hallmarks of greatness, I tell you. And so I acted.

"I have had some rather fruitful investigations this afternoon," I lied, and my voice sounded unnaturally loud in the stillness of contemplative chewing. "Very interesting indeed."

Lord Huffsworthy grimaced. "I can't imagine the police are in need of assistance Mr. Spiffington," he said. "It would be more proper for you to await the conclusion of their investigation, instead of muddying the waters." He bit a moody broccoli.

"But I find I have anticipated their conclusions," I replied.

"Oi, what does that mean?" asked Fitchly Skorjenhensen, ever the subtle conversationalist.

"It means, my good horseman, that I have discovered the link between Dobbins and the two murders. Dobbins actually committed the first murder at the urging of another, and that Other murdered Dobbins to keep him from talking."

"Even had you proof," said Lord Huffsworthy, "that hardly is original or helpful. It does not tell us who the other murderer is." He looked around the table, as if expecting someone to leap up and accost us all with a bread knife.

"Ah, but I can do that as well. We know the identity of the murderer," I said triumphantly. "Don't we Moony, old boy?"

I admit it was a bit of a gamble to rely on Moony like that. But bless his dim little heart he comes through in a pinch. He looked somewhat confused for a moment, which wasn't anything like a giveaway for old Moony, and then said, "Oh. Rather!"

"So it would be best for the murderer if he would just give himself up. I plan on revealing what I know to Chief Inspector Pail as soon as I can get a hold of him."

"Why don't you just tell us who it is?" asked Fitchly Skorjenhensen, the inconvenient beast.

"Because," said Signor MacGregor, "that-a would cause a-panic and a-general turmoil. Mr. Spiffington, he wants-a do it peaceful."

Lord Huffsworthy said, "What if *you* did it, Mr. Spiffington? What if this is bluster designed to conceal your own part in these horrible occurrences?"

"Bluster?" I said, "Bluster? The Spiffington blood shrinks from the idea of bluster. We are a blusterless race if ever one walked the earth. Bluster would be as repulsive to a Spiffington as—"

"We understand, Mr. Spiffington. You express you are not blustering."

"Just so, your Lordship. I know what I know." And here I looked shrewdly at them all.

"I think, Mr. Spiffington, that if you know who the murderer is, then you should reveal it. Surely there are enough of us here to subdue the fiend until the police can intervene."

"We could call the constables in to be at the ready," said Moony excitedly.

"Yes, thank you, Moony," I said. "You are indeed a great help." Moony smiled goofily.

"Perhaps we should adjourn to the library," said Lord Huffsworthy, "and bring a few constables with us."

So we did. On the way to the library, Moony whispered, "Who is it, Reggie?"

I returned his sibilance. "I don't bloody know, Moony! I was bluffing! I hoped the real murderer would give himself away when I spoke!"

"Oh. Did he?"

"No, Moony, he did not. And now I have to reveal that I don't know anything."

"Then why did you adjourn us to the library?"

"Well, I am now hoping the murderer panics and doesn't show in the library."

"Oh. Do you think that's likely?"

"I honestly have no idea, Moony."

"This doesn't seem to be a very well thought out plan, Reggie."

"Thank you, Moony. You have been invaluable."

We arrived in the library, where I was unsurprised at the total failure of my plan. No one was missing, and three constables had joined us, alerted by Lord Huffsworthy. The group took chairs and sofas facing me, expectant that I would soon enlighten them. I stood looking at them, and felt as completely at a loss as I can ever remember feeling. Even when Lady Constance Giblet's father caught me hanging from the ivy outside her window wearing a flannel nightgown with my trousers tied to my head with twine, I had an explanation at the ready. But now, not a sausage. I opened my mouth to speak. It was probably my imagination, but everyone in the room seemed to lean forward and hold their breath as they awaited my next utterance.

I often wonder what I would have said. But fate intervened. And as is so often the case, fate looked at that moment remarkably like my man Pelham. This angel of deliverance entered the room, stepped nimbly over to me and whispered in my ear.

"Sir, you are wanted on the telephone."

"Ah, good man, Pelham," I returned in the same hushed tone. Then, louder, I said, "Oh, dash it all! Unfortunately, my friends, I am called away by the telephone!"

A general groan. Lord Huffsworthy said, "The telephone? You're about to reveal the identity of the murderer! An event which was doubtful, I grant you, but which you have promised and must now deliver!"

"I'm afraid I can't take the time at present, your Lordship. I need to take a rather pressing call. I shouldn't be surprised if this call is in relation to my ongoing investigations here at the Hall. I may be some time. I can't imagine you'll want to wait." And I stepped into the hall.

"Thank you, Pelham, that was brilliant!"

"Sir?"

"Your little ruse just then. Saved me no end of embarrassment."

"Ruse, sir?"

"Oh. You mean there is someone on the telephone for me?"

"Yes, sir. Chief Inspector Pail has rung for you. I told him you would not be a moment."

"Oh. Then lead away, my good man."

The telephone was on a small table in the hallway. As I lifted the receiver to my ear, I was aware Lord Huffsworthy had come out into the hallway.

"Mr. Spiffington," he said, somewhat severely.

"Half a moment, your Lordship," I said, "I've just got to consult with the Chief Inspector." I waited for him to return to the library, but he stood there in a manner that suggested permanence of the geological variety. I spoke into the telephone.

"Hi-ho, Spiffington here."

"Mr. Spiffington," said Pail's voice, "we are releasing Miss Borogove shortly. I wanted to make sure someone would be here to provide her with transportation back to Huffsworthy Hall."

I thought about time and moonrise. "Well, I'm not sure, Chief Inspector. Couldn't you bring her?"

He made a sound which I cannot accurately transcribe. "I'm not a bloody chauffer! You were so keen to have Miss Borogove released—you come here and get her!"

"Well, I'm rather busy at the moment, Chief Inspector."

"What the devil are you busy with?"

"I am, sort of, well. I sort of told the assembled inhabitants of the Hall that I would reveal the identity of the murderer."

"You did what?"

"It was . . ." I looked over my shoulder to where Lord Huffsworthy was watching me. I lowered my voice. "It was a bluff. I thought I could flush out the killer by means of a cunning ruse."

"Good grief, my blood pressure." said Pail. "Mr. Spiffington, may I say rather emphatically that you are not to say anything to anyone about the murder cases under investigation at Huffsworthy Hall? Is that clear, Mr. Spiffington?"

"I think all private citizens are entitled to talk about whatever they—"

"NOT. A. WORD. Can you hear that short and simple command, Mr. Spiffington? NOT. A. WORD. Or else you shall be arrested for obstruction of justice, or impersonating a police officer, or just being an uppity git. I can fill out the paperwork afterward. NOT. A. WORD."

"I am to understand you do not wish me to discuss the case?"

"Have someone come to the station and retrieve Miss Borogove within the hour. Good night, Mr. Spiffington." He retreated into dial tone.

I hung up. Lord Huffsworthy looked at me expectantly, which I felt to be an imposition. I restrained myself, however, and explained the situation.

"Chief Inspector Pail has requested I do not reveal what I know."

"Has he?" asked his Lordship, rather irritatingly, since I had just expressly said that was the case. "Then we have no need to remain assembled?"

"You have surmised correctly, your Lordship."

Lord Huffsworthy stepped to the door of the library, opened it, and then spoke in an unnecessarily loud voice. "Mr. Spiffington has nothing to tell us after all. It was apparently all wind and nonsense." I felt the groan from within. Lord Huffsworthy shot me a glance calculated to remove any illusions I might have as to his adding me to the will, and stalked dolefully away. The rest of the assemblage filtered out of the library behind him. Moony stopped and shook his head.

"Fancy a scotch in the smoking room, Reggie?" he asked. "Arabella is going to bed early. Her nerves, poor thing."

"Yes, old man, that sounds just about right. I'll be turning in early myself tonight, I believe, but I shall quaff a rocky concoction with you first. Go on ahead, and I'll join you in a moment."

"Right ho, Reggie." And away went he.

"Pelham," I said.

"Yes, sir?"

"I need you to go to the local holding tank and retrieve Mimsy."

"Sir? I should remind you of the time."

"Yes, Pelham, but she needs retrieval, and at this point I don't know who is or isn't a killer. Except Moony, and he doesn't drive. I shall be fine. Look for my clothes in the clearing later this evening. I'll see you in the morning."

"As you wish, sir."

"Please, tell me I'll see you in the morning, Pelham. This morning is not something I'd like to repeat."

"I shall make every endeavor, sir."

"Thank you, Pelham."

My man went to accoutre himself before going for the car. I stopped and straightened my tie in the hall mirror. I had roughly an hour and a quarter before moonrise. I could have a drink and then leave via the French doors in the smoking room, hopefully avoiding the posted constables. It had been a decidedly mortifying evening, and by jingo I deserved a scotch. I walked the length of the hall and entered the smoking room, turning to pull the heavy door closed behind me.

I just had time to remark on the dim light and to wonder why Moony was slumped across the billiard table before the blow landed on the back of my skull. And then the light got quickly dimmer, and I began my own slumping.

Chapter Fourteen

I noticed two things immediately upon awakening—I was not a wolf, which meant less than an hour had passed, and a strong smell of horse shit. I apologize for the overtly Anglo-Saxon nature of my language, but since the horse apples in question were just in front of my preternaturally sensitive nose, I feel the need for adequate linguistic force to express the full reality. I was lying on what appeared to be hay, and the back of my head throbbed, if I may venture an anthropomorphism, as if it had made up its mind to achieve Guinness Book status for longevity in throbbing. I regretted sitting up, but at least I could see the lay of the land.

As you may have guessed, clever reader that you are, I was in the stables, lying on the main floor at the back. In fact, as I repositioned myself, I found my back pressed against the rear wall of the stable, underneath the hayloft. A few feet from me, also lying on the straw-strewn floorboards, was Moony Huffsworthy, who was still sampling the delights of the unconscious. Further away on my right, the opposite side from Moony, was Arabella Biscuit. Arabella was chained to the thick wooden column that supported the front right corner of the hayloft. The chain encircled her neck and both wrists. She had apparently been struck on the side of the head and there were blood and tears streaking her face. She was awake, but had not yet seen me move, as her eyes were fixed on the other occupant of the stables.

Fitchly Skorjenhensen was busy by the stable doors. He had a can of petrol in his hands and was splashing the stuff all over some bales of hay stacked by the stalls. He looked much larger than usual, but perhaps that was the effect of the whopping great bruise that had blossomed on the back on my head like a purple foxglove (I have the soul of a poet, even in extremity). The big Cockney Swede was calm and methodical in his task, soaking each stack in a most thorough manner. Soon the smell of petrol vied with the horse shit for dominance. It was a less than ideal venue.

When Fitchly seemed satisfied with his petrol-flinging, he looked over at us. "Ah," he said, "you're awake are you? I'd have bet your skull was a damn sight thicker than that Huffsworthy boob. And I was right, it seems." He walked in our direction, moving thoughtfully, as if in contemplation of our situation. He seemed in no hurry whatsoever. The stable was lit by three electric lights hung on cords from the central beam. These lights cast weird top-down shadows on Fitchly's already scarred granite block of a face as he passed under each one in turn. He stopped underneath the third one, less than twenty feet from our little *tableau a la hostage*. In the light's electric glare, I could see how wild-eyed he looked, how his skin glistened with the exertion of carrying me and Moony from the smoking room, probably by the very French doors I had planned to use in my own escape from the house. He looked murderous, which is I suppose the heart of the matter.

"It didn't have to be like this, you know," he said, shaking his head at us sadly, maniacally. "You could have just left it alone and it would have all been over and done with in a day or two."

"No it wouldn't, Fitchly. Pail and Mutton would have found you out, you know. Dobbins was rather clumsily dispatched. Eventually even Mutton would have seen you were the one. And, if I may ask, what are you hoping to achieve with this rather bucolic kidnapping?"

"What am I hoping to achieve?"

"Yes, Fitchly, you've grasped the question nicely. What are you hoping to achieve?"

"Just you watch it, Spiffington. You've been up my nose ever since you tried to run down my Abercrombie. I've about had it up to here with your snooty airs. What I am hoping to achieve," he delivered this further repetition in an unnecessary and unflatteringly inaccurate approximation of my Cambridge-bred accent, "is making sure you don't peach on me to the police."

"I would think I'd have rather more to tell the police at this juncture, Fitchly. My list of complaints grows by the moment, in fact."

"I intend," continued Skorjenhensen, "to set the stables on fire and burn you all to death while I watch from outside."

Arabella began crying. I looked at her, and then at the unconscious Moony. I realized perhaps barbed wit was not my ally. Unfortunately, that left appeals to logic or emotion, neither of which were the ideal approach to Fitchly Skorjenhensen's apparently deranged mind.

"That hardly seems calculated to absolve you of crime, Fitchly. I may be off base here, I'm not a policeman, but would not your watching us burn up with the stables seem to imply guilt? At least through inaction?"

"Why, Mr. Spiffington. I had no idea you were in the stables. Why would I? I simply came out to check on my horse and saw the fire. I dashed in and rescued Abercrombie, which I will do in half a moment, and got out as fast as I could. It never occurred to me to check for other people in the smoke. Why, I thought everyone was in the house like the police had asked." He smiled with his big head while he said this, his voice oily with petrol.

"They will wonder why we were here, then."

"I have no idea why you did this, Mr. Spiffington. Perhaps you were so upset by your role in the murders that you felt the need to do yourself in, taking your co-conspirators with you. I don't understand the mind of a madman. You're crazy, aren't you? No telling why you do what you do."

It was a fairly good plan, actually. I wouldn't have expected it from him. Arabella continued to cry. She said, "Fitchly, this is insane. Why are you doing this? I thought we were friends!"

Fitchly drew in breath. "Friends? Is that what we were, Arabella?"

"Well, if not friends, then I thought at least we had an understanding. Why did you help me yesterday if you were planning to kill me?"

"I wasn't planning to kill you when I helped you this morning, Arabella. Things are quite different now. But when you think about it, this is all because of you, ain't it?"

"Me? How is this about me? You killed my father for me?"

"Now, Arabella, let's not say what ain't true. I never killed no father of yours."

"Maybe not," I interjected, "but you set Dobbins to it, didn't you? You told him to do it."

"But that's not the same thing at all, Mr. Spiffington. Not at all." He looked back at Arabella. "I loved you, Arabella. I know you never loved me, never thought I was good enough. And I'll own I never understood why Sir Lionel wanted me to marry you; he was so got up about being high and mighty, why would he want some low-class crook like me for the daughter of the house?"

"Perhaps he just found you charming," I said.

"I'd appreciate you shutting your gob, Mr. Nosy Parker," he said viciously, and then continued in his previous tone of dreamy thoughtfulness. "Friday night it all came clear. I mean, first I had to deal with the *complete and utter shattering of everything I ever thought I knew about the world*," he took a moment, "but then I realized. He thought *you* weren't good enough for a regular high society chap. You were a flippin' *werewolf*. He needed some dumb ox of a henchman to pawn you off on. And that was me."

"No, Fitchly," said Arabella, "that's never what you were. I know you aren't—"

"Barking orders at me all the time, using me like a bloody tool. And then when I saw you chained up like that, I didn't know what. Even when I saw what, what you are, there's no need to treat a living creature like that. Something snapped, Arabella."

"I understand, Fitchly," she said. "It was more than anyone could have sanely handled."

"So I went to Dobbins and I said, 'I know a way we can both be rid of this little blighter.' And Dobbins told me where to find them flowers. That was because of you, Arabella."

"Then why undo that now?" I asked.

"Oi, what do you mean, you nancy?"

"Well, it hardly makes sense to commit several crimes to protect Arabella if you're just going to turn around and kill her."

"Things is different, ain't they Mr. Spiffington? You had to keep poking that nose of yours into things. You found out about Dobbins and I had to get rid of him. Then you said you and Mr. Huffsworthy knew who the killer was, and I knew I had to get rid of you two. Who would take care of Arabella with Huffsworthy gone? No, there's no real way a *werewolf* is gonna live in modern England. It's better for her, for everybody." Arabella was crying again, looking at the ground.

"But you say you loved her, Fitchly. Surely—"

"It's the same with horses," he said. "Sometimes even when you love a horse, it's got to be put down, if that's the best way to stop it suffering."

"But—"

"Just shut up now. I got to be going, before she starts to change. You might want to stay away from her, Mr. Spiffington, unless you want to get savaged before you burn up." He turned away from us and walked back toward the front of the stables. As he did, I slid over to Arabella and leaned back against the post to which she was chained. While Fitchly was busy opening Abercrombie's stall, I began trying to quietly unknot the links of chain Fitchly had looped around Arabella's wrists. I whispered while I worked.

"How long until moonrise do you think?"

"I don't know," she said back in the same hissing undertone, "It can't be long. He doesn't know about you?"

"No, he doesn't." I succeeded in getting Arabella's hands free, and left her to work on her neck. My main concern was preventing Fitchly from setting match to hay. I didn't know how to get Moony out if the fire actually got started. So I did the most reasonable thing I could think of—I ran full-tilt at Fitchly while his back was turned.

I don't know if I've had occasion during this narrative to mention that Fitchly Skorjenhensen was a larger than average person. He was so very large as to seem architectural in origin. I think my sprinting toward that fleshy wall in an attempt to save us all was an act of purest optimism, if "optimism" can be used to generally stand in for any term denoting silliness or suicide. Once, due to circumstances best left unstated but which involved an attractive young woman, her severe-visaged chaperone, a tinned calf tongue, and a terrier called Nigel, I ran into the brick wall surrounding Highgate Cemetery at something like fifteen miles an hour. The impact I experienced when I reached Fitchly Skorjenhensen recalled that incident so evocatively that I tasted tongue.

Fitchly had gotten Abercrombie out of the stall and was working with the bridle as I came careening into the vast expanse of his back. I'm not sure what sort of reaction I expected, but his turning and beginning to laugh was particularly humiliating, given I just had the breath knocked out of me. Fitchly hit me hard in the jaw, a real prizefighter uppercut, and as I hit the ground on my tailbone my teeth made an audible clacking.

"You daft bugger," said the big man, "stay on the bloody ground where I put you!" And then he cuffed me on the ear, knocking me sideways into the straw. I was still struggling to sit up straight as he pulled a matchbox from his shirt pocket and struck a flame. He tossed it into the hay beside the stalls and pulled Abercrombie toward the door. The hay bales lit up like Piccadilly Circus and I panicked. I launched myself again at the pair of them. I can't recommend repeated concussion as a stimulant for clear thinking.

I was saved by the moon. I spun around and fell to the ground again—lots of ground-hitting this evening—and began to change. I heard the cloth tearing as I split my clothes. I could see Arabella from where I sat. She had freed herself and crawled over to attempt to awaken Moony, and she was contorting on the ground as I now began to do. Fitchly did not see she was free of her chains, because he had eyes only for me.

"What the bloody hell?" he eloquently espoused. "*Two* of you?"

And then I was a wolf. Once again, events shifted into a wolf-in-the-moment perspective—action and reaction was all I could muster, but I had already been in that sort of a mindset, what with being knocked twice in the head and being threatened with personal arson. An explosion of action (not an actual explosion, you understand, though the hay and the wall behind it was burning at a fair clip), I growled my best growl and leapt for Fitchly's throat.

As a side note, I can't tell you how satisfying it is to leap for someone's throat, particularly if that someone has been irritating for several days. Skorjenhensen mitigated that satisfaction somewhat by raising his arm, and my first closing of the jaws merely scratched his forearm. I was quick to push forward, however, and got a good tearing bite at the jawline. Missed the jugular, I presume, since the amount of blood produced was less than should be expected, but I certainly gave him a nasty wound. He gave a gurgling yelp and I gave another growl. By this point Arabella had crossed the stable to join me, and the two of us sized up our quarry preparatory to having another go.

Sadly, such was not to be. I have no compunction in expressing my fervent desire to be an agent of dispatch for Fitchly Skorjenhensen, at least in that instinct-driven moment. But fate had a more interesting plan for the mad Swede. Urged on by the flaming walls and the sudden presence of two wolves, Abercrombie had been doing his best to lose what passed for a mind in the huge horse's head. My transformation had induced him into rearing and whinnying with abandon as panicked fear held sway. Just as Arabella and I coiled our lupine muscles for a final spring, Abercrombie did the deed for us. Rearing up again onto his hind legs, the big stallion's pawing front hoof struck Fitchly full on the forehead, splitting his skull with a sound clearly audible over the roar of the flames. The big man fell under the horse's hooves, and thus ended Fitchly Skorjenhensen.

The door to the stables burst open at this point, and Pelham entered at a run, an overcoat thrown across his upraised arm and face, Mimsy Borogove peering through the smoke behind him. As Pelham moved past us, Arabella and I took the opportunity to dash through the door and into the blessed cool of the night, where we soon lost ourselves among the trees behind the burning building.

Chapter Fifteen

It is disconcerting to awaken outdoors next to the love interest of a dear friend, and if both you and the young lady in question are naked, awkwardness is likely to ensue. I take this as a firm point of etiquette. On this occasion, however, a shared sense of identity and awareness of circumstances mollified the situation. We were quick to turn our eyes away, certainly, though not before an unwarranted and unwelcome confirmation of the Noodle metaphor was burned into my brain. Fortunately for both of us, Pelham was much more punctual this morning, was in fact waiting for us as we reached the clearing. Clothes had been procured for both of us, and we soon were clad and as composed as a swift running of the comb (also thoughtfully provided by Pelham) could render us.

During this rustic toilette, Pelham filled us in on the conclusion of the fiery events of the previous night. Upon entering the blazing stables, Pelham had quickly and accurately assessed the situation, seen that Fitchly was beyond assistance, recognized Arabella and myself as we dashed past him (who else could we be?), and fortunately looked deeper into the smoke to find Moony, still out cold. Pelham had carried him to safety with Mimsy's help. The fire had been put out by the quick-acting constabulary, but the stables would be some weeks in repair.

"Mr. Huffsworthy is presently recovering in his room, attended by the local physician from Huffton-on-Spry. He suffers from smoke inhalation and a nasty concussion, but he is most fortunate in that those are the extent of his injuries."

"My poor Archibald," said Arabella, straightening her stockings. "I shall take care of him. I shall make it all up to him."

"He must have been hit like a ton of what-do-call-its," I said. "He never moved during the whole of that ordeal in the stables."

"I would surmise you were all hit with more than a modicum of force," said Pelham. "You, sir, and Miss Biscuit as well, are better suited to withstanding the blunt strength of someone like Fitchly Skorjenhensen."

"Yes," said Arabella, "especially at this time of month. We're a sturdy breed, Mr. Spiffington."

"What did you tell Mimsy?" I asked. "She must have seen us. And she must have wondered where we were. Crumbs, for that matter, why have the police not wondered where we are?"

"The police are at present searching for you," said Pelham. "I am assisting in the search even now, and volunteered to look in the wooded areas south of the lawn. I anticipate reporting success when I return to the house with you."

"Oh. Good for you, Pelham. Why are we out here, I wonder?"

"I cannot say, sir. If forced to speculate, I would imagine the 'ordeal in the stable,' as you put it, was terrifying. Having managed to escape through a window, it would seem likely you hid in the woods, afraid of returning to the house for fear of Mr. Skorjenhensen."

"That doesn't follow, old bean. The house was crawling with police. Wouldn't we have been more likely to have gone to them?"

"I would have, sir. But given the hysteria to which you are sometimes subject, it is difficult to predict what you will do in a given situation. Rational decisions are not always your forte."

"Given the hysteria—"

"Yes, sir. Attendant, one would assume, on your alcoholism."

"I do wish these explanations of yours didn't always make me appear a dissolute bedlamite, Pelham."

"It is unfortunate, sir. You have my sympathies."

"Arabella is not an alcoholic, I presume?"

"No," said Arabella as she fastened her shoe, "but I am a fragile young woman. It is my nature to be hysterical, especially if a man tells me to be, as you must have."

"That doesn't paint you in the brightest of colors, Arabella."

"Welcome to the world of werewolves, Mr. Spiffington. People will always think badly of you now, but that's preferable to having them think the truth."

"What about Mimsy?" I asked Pelham.

"Miss Borogove is much too shrewd, and much too intimate with you, to believe such a story, sir. I took the liberty of telling her the truth."

"Begod, Pelham! What did she say?"

"She found it at first unlikely, but seems undeterred in her desire to see you."

"Well, that's good. Isn't it?"

"I am loath to speculate on the motives of the fairer sex in regard to yourself, sir."

"Thank you, Pelham."

I did not get to speak with Mimsy immediately. Chief Inspector Pail demanded my time at once and seemed at first reticent to accept my version of events. However, after hearing from Constable Wiggins about his encounter with me as I wandered naked through the garden on Sunday morning, he had to admit that coupled with my behavior throughout the weekend, all signs seemed to point to me being a crazy but harmless drunkard. I suppose I should have thanked Pelham, but I lacked the motivation. Arabella and I recounted the bulk of the evening's events, implying Abercrombie's panic was fire-induced, which wasn't completely untrue. The irrefutable evidence of Fitchly's body, badly burned but also demonstrably hoof-trampled, confirmed the truth of our tale. Later the police, searching the man's room, would discover a note Fitchly had written to himself: "Foxglove. Purple. Bell-shaped. Back of garden by the bench." This seemed to sew it up.

"Mr. Spiffington," offered Pail as a parting comment, "I'd suggest staying in London from here on out. We country-folk don't hold with the hoity-toity playboy types. We'll all be more comfortable if you don't visit too often."

London was top on my list of things I'd like to see after my weekend at Huffsworthy Hall. Or nearly the top. I needed first to find Mimsy Borogove. Alas, on my way to find her, I was waylaid again, this time by Pelham, who had someone else in tow.

"Sir, if I may arrest your progress momentarily, Signor Reynaldo MacGregor wishes a word with you." And indeed, the Scottish-Italian tenor presented himself with a deep bow.

"I give-a you my card, Mr. Spiffington," he said, and then followed word with action. The card was of a thick cream-colored paper, edged with black and containing only his name and address:

> Reynaldo MacGregor
> 27 Cheyne Walk
> Chelsea
> London SW3

"When you ready, you come and-a see me, Mr. Spiffington."

"And why would I do that, Signor MacGregor? Just what is this about?"

"Itsa about wolves, Mr. Spiffington. And-a the people who become wolves. Take this." He handed me a leather-bound book. "You read that book. And then you come-a for tea, yes?"

"I shall have to check my diary," I said. "I am quite busy."

"Oh, you make-a time for me," he said, and then bowed again before leaving the hall by the front door. I could see his chauffer standing by his car on the gravel beyond.

"Well, Pelham, have you any thoughts?"

"I cannot extend a definitive answer, sir. I have not encountered Signor MacGregor beyond here at Huffsworthy Hall and on the stage with the National Opera. He seems to know things that aren't immediately obvious."

"Should I be worried, Pelham?"

"I cannot say, sir. Perhaps it would not be imprudent to pursue that matter further."

"Take his invitation to tea, you mean?"

"As you say, sir. That would be the speediest manner in which to uncover the mystery. What is the book, if I may ask?"

We looked at it together. It was *The Book of Were-wolves*, by the Reverend Sabine Baring-Gould. Looked frightfully old and lengthy. I gave it to Pelham to pack with my other things.

Mimsy Borogove was in the drawing room, looking radiant against the blasphemous upholstery of a paisley chaise-lounge. She stood when I entered and stepped to me in a most satisfying manner, taking both of my hands in hers.

"Reggie—I've been so worried!"

"There was naught to worry about, my dear. Once you and Pelham opened the door, I was as good as safe."

She dropped my hands and stepped back to look at me seriously. "But Reggie, this astonishing story that Pelham has told me. Are you saying it is true? That those two beasts I saw in the stable were . . . you and Arabella?"

"He spoke the truth, Mimsy. It is difficult to comprehend, I know. I am still grappling with the implications myself. It was only Friday evening I saw the drapes of reality thrown back as it were."

"Friday night? You mean the dog you said had bitten you was—?"

"Arabella Biscuit. She has apologized."

"Apologies seem superfluous, Reggie. I'm finding this rather hard to digest. This is the stuff of novels. And not the sort that I write."

"I have learned a healthier respect for pulp fiction during the past two days, certainly. And Rin Tin Tin. Mimsy, I understand if you are horrified by my affliction. You have no obligations to me. I am sorry to have never picnicked with you."

Mimsy stepped close again and touched my face. "Reggie. I am fascinated. If this is actually a true thing, then it changes the entire way I view the world. Horrifying? Yes, I suppose so. But I spent Saturday with you and didn't find you any less the man I know you to be. In fact, in the library Saturday evening—"

"I fear my overt demonstration of affection Saturday evening may have sprung from my newly acquired wolfish nature, Mimsy."

"Oh. Oh! Wolves have great . . . *appetites?*"

"Voracious."

"That's, that's astonishing, Reggie. And intriguing in the extreme. I don't think we have to cancel all plans of a picnic, darling." She pressed close to me for a moment, and pressed her lips to mine. "But," she continued, "I am afraid I have to leave this morning. I have a meeting with my publisher this afternoon in London."

"I'll be leaving as well, I believe. I'm not as keen on Huffsworthy Hall as I once was."

"But, you'll be in London, yes?"

"I have no immediate plans to be elsewhere."

"Perhaps a picnic in the park? One evening soon?"

"I think that would be a consummation devoutly to be wished, my dear. Here's my number." I handed her a card. "Please call me. It will give me reason not to dread the telephone."

I had but to look in on Moony before leaving. I sent Pelham to load the baggage and bring the car around. I wanted to leave before breakfast; I couldn't face another meal at the Huffsworthy table. I was on my way to the stairs when I encountered Lord Huffsworthy on the way down. I had hoped to avoid the man. The only reason to speak with him would have been to thank him for a lovely weekend, and after what had transpired, well I mean to say.

"Mr. Spiffington," said Lord Huffsworthy, "I am glad to see you safely returned after your trials last night. It is truly ghastly to consider what almost happened to my Archibald."

"There is no need for thanks, your Lordship," I said. "It was touch and go for a while, obviously. I am merely grateful we have all come out of it alive."

"I have no intention of thanking you, Mr. Spiffington. I am astounded you would expect such sentiments from me. You ran from the scene, all but kidnapping my son's fiancé, leaving Archibald behind at the hands of that brute Skorjenhensen. If Miss Borogove and your manservant had not arrived when they did, my son would have been listed as a third casualty in the horrid debacle this weekend has devolved into. You are a coward, sir, and if Chief Inspector Pail had not informed me of your raging addiction to the demon alcohol, I would throw you out of my house this instant. As it is, I merely ask you, quite forcefully, to leave before the day is out and not to return unless you have spent much time with a doctor who deals with lushes."

"Ah. I see. I thank you for your recommendations, your Lordship. I will endeavor to conquer my love of the bottle. Perhaps you could lay a bet on my odds for recovery?"

"Mr. Spiffington, try not to injure yourself as you exit. I wish nothing to delay your departure."

Moony was propped on pillows waited on by Arabella Biscuit, who sat close by the bedside holding his hand and dabbing at his face with a wet handkerchief. Only upon seeing them did the full import of what Lord Huffsworthy had said seize my brain. "Moony," I said, "have you gone and gotten engaged since we've returned?"

Moony blushed. Not becoming. "Reggie—I can't thank you enough. You certainly held up your end of our bargain. I am simply delirious."

"Well, the effects of smoke inhalation are notorious, Moony, old man. *My* end of the bargain? What was your end of the bargain?"

"A weekend in the country at our estate, of course."

"I could accuse you of reneging, Moony, if you didn't looked so dashed happy."

"We're to be married before the end of the summer, Reggie. I do hope you'll come!"

"Oh, yes," said Arabella, looking away from Moony for the first time. "Please say you'll be at our wedding, Reggie. I feel we owe you so much."

"If the wedding is somewhere other than Huffsworthy Hall, I wouldn't miss it," I said. "You make a lovely couple."

"We are so in love," said Moony. "Sharing the extraordinary events of these past three days have made us so close." They began gazing afresh.

"Yes, we've all gone through the fire, as it were," I said. "I will go now, and leave you two to bask in the glow. Send me an invitation."

Arabella followed me into the hallway and spoke in a low voice. "Mr. Spiffington, I cannot express what I feel. These few days have been so full of horror and joy I haven't the words. I assume you will stay in touch? We too have shared more than a little."

"I am sure we will have a lot to say to one another over the years. I will have questions, I've no doubt. Arabella, does Moony know?"

She glanced back toward the door, through which we could see Moony lying weakly under the coverlet. "No, Mr. Spiffington. I don't know how to tell him. I know I must. He is such a sweet trusting boy." She smiled at him, and he waggled his fingers at her.

"He is," I said. "Be worthy of his trust. Moony won't desert you, Arabella. He may not be a thinker—who among us is?—but he is loyal. Tell him before the wedding."

She looked thoughtfully at me, surprised I'm sure at the wisdom which I spouted. "I will," she said. "I will. Thank you, Reggie."

At long last I was in the roadster. Pelham was at the wheel, and I leant back against the leather and watched the landscape roll by. The fields were a brilliant green, and the sky was as near to cloudless blue as could be wished. I felt changed, and I didn't mind saying it.

"Pelham?"

"Yes, sir?"

"I don't mind saying I feel changed."

"Indeed, sir?"

"Yes, Pelham. Changed. I am a changed man."

"You refer to the fact that you are a werewolf, sir?"

"I suppose that's part of it, Pelham. But it doesn't cover the whole field, if you see what I mean."

"You feel a moral strength arising from your newfound ability to stand your ground against murderers, lords, baronets, and chefs, perhaps?"

"I can't say that completely encompasses it, Pelham."

"In what practical ways do you foresee your perceived change manifesting itself, sir?"

"Oh, I don't know, Pelham. I may be less likely to lie in of a morning. Perhaps I shall be friendlier to the machinations and accusations of my aged grandfather, the Not-So-Honorable Hammerthorpe Q. Spiffington. It is not implausible I may take up charity work, or spend more time with animals."

"Indeed, sir?"

"I can't say for certain. Something about being a wolf, Pelham. I feel a grand adventure beginning. Not just that I'll spend part of each month howling under the full moon, or that Mimsy Borogove finds my lycanthropic nature enticing. Something larger. I feel almost as if my immersion into my animal nature has somehow widened my humanity in ways I can't yet know."

"You are waxing quite metaphysical, sir. I am nearly speechless."

"Unlike you, Pelham."

"I did qualify the adjective, sir. It may perhaps be a fortuitous time to share with you the telegram I received at Huffsworthy Hall this morning whilst you spoke with Miss Borogove."

"A telegram? For me? Who knew I was at the Hall?"

"Apparently someone did, sir. I have it here." He produced a telegram from an inner pocket and handed it to me. I opened it with my penknife and perused the contents.

"Good god, Pelham. My aged grandfather, Hammerthorpe Q. Spiffington, has tracked me down like a bloodhound. He writes to inform me he has arranged dinner at his house in town tonight for me and a party which will include Lady Mildred Spinoza."

"Perhaps your grandparent feels this would give you ample opportunity to explain to Lady Spinoza the circumstances under which you failed to keep your appointment with her last Thursday."

"He says as much in his surprisingly long-winded telegram."

"A perfect occasion for you to put your newly discovered changes to the test, sir."

"Yes, Pelham. Yes, indeed."

I contemplated the green and pleasant fields. Pelham drove with an enviable efficiency. I looked at him. "Pelham?"

"Yes, sir?"

"I feel it would be an insult to the changes I have experienced to test them so soon. Lycanthropy is a tiring business."

"I quite understand, sir."

"Perhaps you could reply for me?"

"I will explain that you have been detained longer than expected at Huffsworthy Hall and have been engaged for dinner or charity work for the remaining evenings this week."

"Pelham, you are invaluable."

"Thank you, sir. I do try my best."

ACKNOWLEDGMENTS

Incorporating as it does so many of the types of characters and stories I love, I expected writing this novel to be a joy. I wasn't disappointed, but I wasn't prepared for the additional joy of working with so many talented and helpful folks as it got cleaned up, polished, and ready to meet the world. First and foremost, I want to express my deepest gratitude to my friend and editor Jen Woods, whose belief in my novel and me are matched only by her unwavering eye and attention to every detail. I am blessed to be in such dazzlingly capable hands. My appreciation also to Brian Esminger and Lindsey Alexander at Typecast, as well as to Eric Woods at Firecracker Press for helping the book look as gorgeous as it does.

I am also indebted to early readers who gave valuable feedback during the drafting and revision process—Amy Reeves, Heather Smith, and Tracy Price all gave honest reactions and advice in this regard, and thus each left their mark on the final product. My wife Gwyn offered deeper and repeated readings, and served as general in-progress respondent. I also got helpful advice from my Official Poison Consultant, Angela Partain, who gleefully offered several gruesome options for dispatching Sir Lionel, with nasty details of the death process induced by each. Really she enjoyed it a little too much.

I always love working with the gracious and gifted Ali LaRock, who has once again created images that seem to have been pulled directly from my fevered brain. I hope she will be drawing my words for years to come.

And for supporting me in every endeavor through the unfettered giving of love, feedback, space, time, and environment, I am as ever astonished and grateful for my family: Ian, Eva, and Gwyn.

Jamieson Ridenhour is the creator of the award-winning short fairy-tale horror film *Cornerboys*, as well as the editor of the Valancourt edition of J. Sheridan Le Fanu's *Carmilla*. His fiction and poetry has appeared in *Strange Horizons*, *Weird Tales*, and *The Lumberyard*, among others. The South Carolina native now lives in Bismarck, ND, where he writes poetry about movie monsters and murder-mysteries with werewolves in them. He also plays wicked lead guitar with Bismarck-based rock and roll band Blind Mice, lectures on vampires and Charles Dickens (though not at the same time), and generally frolics on the plains. He lives with his wife Gwyn and their children Ian and Eva.

Arabella Biscuit

Pelham